I0788411

Fae Hunter

Tangled Fae: Book One

Sarah K. L. Wilson

Published by Sarah K. L. Wilson, 2019.

This is a work of fiction. Similarities to real people, places, or events are entirely coincidental.

FAE HUNTER

First edition. September 4, 2019.

Written by Sarah K. L. Wilson.

For Cale.

Other Books by Sarah K. L. Wilson

Dragon School Series
First Flight
Initiate
The Dark Prince
The Ruby Isles
Sworn
Dusk Covenant
First Message
Warring Promises
Prince of Dragons
Dark Night
Bright Hopes
Mark of Loyalty
Dire Quest
Ancient Allies
Pipe of Wings
Dragon Piper
Dust of Death
Troubled War
Starie Night
Ascendant Light
Dragon Chameleon Series
Rogue's Quest
Paths of Deception
City of Ice
Mist of Power
Silver Eyes
World of Legends
Chase the Moon
Shadow Quest

Creeping Darkness
Golem Siege
Memory of Mountains
Color of Victory
Dragon Tide Series
Dragonlet
Dragon Staff
Desperate Flight
Bubbles of Hope
Waves of Destiny
Tides of Change
Keys of Power
Rock Eaters
Underworld
Chosen One
The Unweaving Chronicles Series
Teeth of the Gods
Lightning Strikes Twice
Thunder Rattles High
Bridge of Legends Series
Summernight
Dawnspell
Autumngale
Winterfast
Springhatch

BOOK ONE

When the barriers were weak, they came in. They were smoke and mirrors. They were dust and mist. They stole into our minds as smoke under a door. They slid through our thoughts as oil in water. We welcomed them. We wanted them. We were them.

-Tales of the Faewald

Chapter One

His smile was both angelic and darkly sinful. It made my young heart flutter like a jar of butterflies.

"I knew you were real," Hulanna said, reaching toward him. The flower crown in her dark red curls had fallen over one eye – a crown almost identical to mine. It gave her a look of surprised innocence.

His smile deepened.

My sister and I were both breathless from our dancing and laughter, petals and crushed grass strewn around our feet like offerings. Our eyes were wide and cheeks bright with excitement.

Dancing around the Star Stones was just daring trouble to find you – if you believed the old wives in our village. No one I'd ever heard of had dared to try it. No one except for us.

"I just knew you would come," her face practically glowed with excitement as her adoring gaze sought his.

It wasn't supposed to *work*. It was just a silly prank. I wasn't supposed to call whatever it had called.

He wasn't human. That was the first thing of which I was sure. From the delicate points of his pale ears to the perfect marble planes of his gorgeous face and rippling muscles – a being like that wasn't human. Did I mention that he was shirtless? His light silk vest was open and rippling in the breeze and his tooled-leather boots and brocade breeches hugged his strong form.

I felt my face growing hot. I was trying not to look. Trying to pretend I wasn't studying him from the corner of my eye.

"I dreamed of you," he said to Hulanna with a voice like a clear crystal bell. He crept a step closer. Here in the howling winds of the upland plain between the standing rocks – here in a place as open as open can be, as lonely as lonely can be – his simple step forward seemed intimate.

I glanced back to where the woods ended and the plains began. Some instinct told me I should be in those trees right now. Everything inside me was screaming that I should run, run, run as fast as I could.

But maybe, a tiny voice in my heart said, maybe he really did dream of her. After all, if he said that to you, you'd believe it, wouldn't you? You'd believe anything that dropped from those seductive red lips and that devilish half-smile.

He knows he's charming, doesn't he? The rest of my heart said. Does he practice that adoring look in the mirror or has he just seduced so many women that it's natural to him?

It was the eyes. It was those dark, magnificent eyes that seemed to see all your secrets at once. They dreamed the dreams of devils and angels, suggesting that rays of sunshine could kiss the shadows and create something utterly new. They'd seen things we could barely imagine – things too magical and wonderous for two village girls high in the mountains. They made me want to see all those things, too.

I shook my head to clear it. Since when had I wanted to see magic? I was happy enough with my mountains and my future as the village hunter. I didn't need magic or pale faces and inviting lips.

"You dreamed of *me*?" Hulanna asked, her pale lips parting as if inviting a kiss. She took a step forward so that now she was standing almost inside the circle of rocks, her eyes large and liquid and her body swaying slightly as if she were still dancing the dance we'd used to call him.

What kind of magical creature comes when you call? What's in it for them if their world is so fascinating? Is it a prank? A trick?

Or can dreams really come true?

He held his hands out as if he wanted to touch her – as if he couldn't quite bring himself to do it. As if giving in might break the spell. And the burning adoration in his eyes made me swallow even though it wasn't meant for me.

My face grew hotter. I shouldn't be watching this private moment, should I? If it was real. If it wasn't all a sham – then surely it was private.

But we'd come up here together. Just two sisters sneaking up to the forbidden rocks. And we'd made our crowns and danced the dance of the Shining Ones as we skipped through knee-high flowers of blue and white and gold and we'd laughed and tried to describe how beautiful they would be when they came.

We'd been wrong.

But only because our imaginations were too small. Only because words weren't enough when it came to this being. Words would never be enough.

"Of *you*," he agreed, nodding, and his eyes warmed even more – how was that possible? – as his smile seemed to draw her close. "I've been dreaming of you all my life. My one, true, perfect mate."

Hulanna laughed just a little nervously. "That can't be me. Can it?"

The way she looked down coyly, the way her dark lashes made fans over her cheeks and her rapid breathing made her chest rise and fall so quickly that eyes were drawn to her form – well, maybe she didn't know what that might do to a man. I had a pretty good idea. I'd been watching boys' eyes get big around Hulanna all my life. She was the pretty one. The dreamy one. The one everyone wanted to know.

But she hadn't been good when she convinced me to come here with her.

Our parents were going to be so angry when we got home. Furious.

"I had a dream," she had said while we were herding the goats to the high pasture this morning. "And it was of a place where gemstones are more common than wildflowers."

"Sounds cold," I'd said, twitching my rod to remind the goats to keep going.

"Of a place where everyone is beyond beautiful – like the angels of heaven."

"I hate beautiful people," I said, prodding one of the goats with my finger to move his stubborn behind down the path. "They don't bother being anything else. They aren't funny or smart or wise or interesting – they're just pretty because that's all they need to be."

"The food there was all ambrosia and truffles," she sighed.

"Have you ever had ambrosia? I mean, the bards talk about it as if it's amazing, but what if it's just goat's milk? Maybe it's all a scheme that some ambrosia dealer down on the lowlands uses to get people wanting something that's actually awful."

But she wasn't having any of my cynical attitude today.

"There was a prince there – the most beautiful prince in the world with raven black hair to his shoulders and huge green eyes and corded, rippling muscles running down through his core, and ..."

"Let's stop the image there," I said dryly. "The only core I'm interested in right now is the core of the apple waiting for me with my lunch."

"Don't be like that, Allie. Will you come with me to the Star Stones?" she'd asked – no, begged – and she'd turned that look on me. It was the look she was giving him right now. The look that would make you do anything.

"I'm not worthy of you," he was saying to her with those green eyes sparkling in the sunlight and that dark hair curling around his neck and brushing his nose where it fell out of place. But if he really thought that, then why was he here trying to seduce her? He bit his lower lip and reached out a hand, almost touching her – but not – as if he were afraid to taint her with his touch. "Please. Please say I have a little hope."

And he looked like a tortured soul – like her answer could break him to a thousand pieces. She drew in a breath and I saw it catch in her throat.

"Don't," I said – and I broke the spell. I hardly knew why I was speaking at all. There was a magic to this – a magic that told me in a loud voice in my mind that this was none of my affair. I should be silent and small. I ignored the loud voice, whispering. "Don't do it."

His features hardened and for a moment, I saw something feral in them – something like the wild hogs we hunt in the downs – something that would gore you with a tusk as soon as look at you, but Hulanna's eyes were on me.

"Don't you see, Allie?" she said to me, with a pitying look in her eye as if I could never understand this. "We're fated mates. He's the prince of my dreams."

"Nothing's fated," I said uncomfortably, shifting from foot to foot. But I wasn't as certain as I wanted to be, and it showed in my tone. After all, who was I to judge? Maybe he really was the prince of her dreams. Maybe I was just jealous. No perfect man had ever told me that he'd dreamed of me. No imperfect one either, for that matter.

All his perfections only made me conscious of my own imperfections – my hawk nose, too-bright red hair, and sharp features. My less-than-perfect figure. If he ever touched me, he'd find me wanting. But not Hulanna. She was all perfection. When our parents made us, the dice had rolled all in her favor. Twins – but not identical. Never that.

Maybe this sparkly pale creature really would make her happy. But why did it feel like he couldn't? Why did it feel like this was a ruse?

"Our love *is* fated," the being said and from his back, a pair of wings suddenly appeared – ghostly as if they were only half there. They were iridescent in the sun like dragonfly wings. "The love of Lord Cavariel, Prince of Cups and," he tilted his head to the side like he was listening to something, "and Hulanna daughter of the Hunter."

He smiled like he'd just solved a riddle but Hulanna's cheeks were pink as she stood on tiptoes to look at his magnificent wings.

How did he know her name?

"Or at least," and here he bit his lip in a way that shot little thrills through me even though it wasn't aimed at me at all. How could someone so dangerous be so appealing? He made my insides feel like butter even while my mind was screaming that something wasn't right. "It is if she wants it."

"I want it," Hulanna said shyly and a bit breathlessly. She must be feeling the butter thing, too. "It's why I came here today."

She was smiling now – the smile of a girl in the prime of her beauty accepting the invitation of the man of her dreams. A smile of triumph and certainty. A smile of achievement.

Fear rippled through me, tangling with the buttery feeling in a way that confused me.

Because none of this could be real, could it? Because until this afternoon when we arrived here, I'd spent my life in our little village, the daughter of the village hunter. And Hulanna was my twin sister. She wasn't someone fated to marry an otherworldly being. She was just Hulanna.

Oh, I'd heard the tales of the passing tinkers, and farmbards, and monks. I'd heard the firelight tales of the Elders. I'd even read the two books they kept in the school – *Tales of the Faewald* and *History of Zrakterra*. And yes, there were stories of the Shining Ones – of Fae males falling in love with human women, but until this moment, I'd never believed they were true.

"What do I need to do to prove to you that I am yours for the taking?" he asked her, and somehow he seemed even more beautiful than ever with his open hands held out to her and his eyes wide as if his very heart were being offered to her in his hands. His lips were slightly open as if there were a thousand things he'd like to say to her.

"Nothing more," Hulanna said, with a broad grin and before I could call to her to stop, she reached through the Star Stones into the circle that none of us were supposed to cross, and she took his hands and stepped forward into the circle to join him.

The angelic smile on his face widened and he seemed to almost glow as he leaned down to kiss her. It was sweet and beautiful and terrifying all at once and after a moment his kiss turned passionate and hers did as well and I thought that I should look away.

Good thing I didn't. If I had, I wouldn't have seen what happened to Hulanna and no one would have ever known.

With a flash of light, she disappeared, leaving only the shining Prince of Cups.

"You too, little sister?" he asked as his hand reached for me.

"What have you done with her?" I gasped. My face felt cold now, my legs trembling.

"There might be a fated mate for you, too," he said with a wink and then he vanished and another Shining One was there in his place. This one was just as pale, just as green-eyed and just as perfect. But I could feel the feral nature in him even more strongly than I had in Lord Cavariel or whatever fool name the other had given us. Dark tattoos like intricate vines clung to his forearms and tangled up his sides. And the look in his eyes was more triumphant than Hulanna's had been.

"Give her back!" I shouted, but I didn't dare step into the circle,

"Come get her." His teeth were pointed inside his wide grin. And that grin was not nice at all. "Step in the circle."

I spun in place. I needed to get help. Someone would be out there. Someone would help me get her back. They had to.

We hadn't meant any trouble. We'd just been fooling around. Who could have guessed that dancing – just silly dancing! – would have this kind of consequence?

My heart was beating so fast that I couldn't hear his next words, but as I ran, I felt fingers scrape my shoulders and that was all I needed to launch into a faster sprint.

My crown of wildflowers fell from my head, petals flying up as I crushed it underfoot. My vision jarred with each pounding footstep. I stole a look behind my back, my heartbeat roaring in my ears.

He was right there! I was barely ahead of him at all!

His perfect face had transformed from angelic to feral and the look in his eyes was hunger.

I screamed, running, running, but too afraid to look in front of me with his hands so close, those pointed teeth so, so close. The smell of death chased me with him, as if he'd already devoured me. I didn't dare tear my eyes away from him.

I felt pain first, even before I realized I had run into something.

And then everything went dark.

Chapter Two

I woke to a pounding headache and voices. Voices and darkness. I could smell my bed and the pine, cedar, and fermenting goat cheese scent of our home. I sank into the scent, grasping at its familiarity. I'd had a terrible dream. The worst dream possible.

The door banged as it hit the wall. Strange that someone was entering in the dark.

"Have you found her?" my mother's voice sounded desperate, worn to tatters.

"Nowhere." My father sounded exhausted. "We combed everything again. All the woods for miles around. Down the river. Fisher dived the pond at the bottom of the falls. Just in case."

"And there was nothing? No scrap of her dress or ... or anything."

It hadn't been a dream at all. Hulanna had really stepped through the circle and been taken by the Shining Ones and when morning came, I would have to tell my parents. I felt a stab of fear shoot through me and I bit my lip. The house felt strange without her there. Even at night, I could usually hear her breathing in her nearby cot.

"Nothing." Now my father was the one who sounded anguished. "They knew not to go up there. They knew it's forbidden."

"They're young. Young people never believe it when you tell them that something is dangerous. They always think they'll be the exception. Or they don't believe it's dangerous at all."

I hadn't thought it was dangerous. I'd thought it was just legends and superstitions. Kings and Queens were real – though their reigns hardly touched us so far into the mountains. Knights and paladins fought great clashing battles on the plains and even mages were sometimes whispered about. Sometimes tales of those things drifted up to us with traders and merchants. But the Shining Ones – everyone knew that was just superstition. Everyone knew they couldn't actually hurt us. And Hulanna had thought she would be the exception. Mother was right on both counts.

"Sit down, Hunter," she said.

Why were they talking in the dark instead of kindling a light?

"Eat some breakfast. You've been out all night and the sun's already high. You need something to eat."

Wait.

The sun was high?

My breath caught in my throat.

The sun was high, and I couldn't see.

"Mother?" I tried to keep the fear out of my voice, but it was there anyway. It trembled through my voice and shot through my body with bowl-loosening fear.

"Allie!" The relief in my mother's voice was palpable. I heard her rushing toward me, and I thought that maybe I saw an outline of her like a glowing spirit – but she was still all I could see – and I could hardly even see her. What was wrong with my eyes?

She gathered me up in a tight hug and I began to cry, as if the warmth and softness of her embrace had opened up the river of my fear.

"Where's your sister?" My father's voice was tight. Was that him I was seeing, too? Glowing faintly blue and looking strange as if he had been painted on a rock and then smudged with an idle sleeve. "Where's Hulanna?"

"He took her," I said, choking over my own tears. "She asked me to go up to the circle with her and I did, and we danced – "

"No!" My mother's gasp was all horror and loss.

"And then he appeared, and she went with him."

"She went with him? A Shining One?" my father asked, his voice still tight. "Willingly?"

"Yes." My voice trembled as I spoke.

My mother was crying now, too, holding me so tight that it hurt – as if she could make up for losing one girl by holding the other one tighter.

"Your eyes look strange," my father said tightly.

"I ... I can't see a thing," I said, as my mother's sobs came harder.

But I could see – sort of. I could see my parents – they looked like themselves, only pale and bright at the same time and they seemed to jitter when they moved. It gave me a headache to try to focus on them. And I was beginning to see some details of our house. And over top of all of it, I was seeing things I'd never seen before. Tracks on the floor of creatures I'd never seen or heard tell of. Long silver and gold trails in the air that I was certain led to something. And there was something in the attic glowing bright as the sun, calling to me.

What in the world could that be?

Chapter Three

A goat was chewing loudly beside me as I ran a hand idly through its hair. Unsurprisingly, it smelled like goat. If I'd been able to see at all, it would have looked like goat, too. I could see only the faintest image of it – a dull blue that flickered in for only long enough to make me dizzy before it was gone again.

All these faint almost-sights were making my head throb like someone was jamming my mother's sewing scissors into it. I gritted my teeth against a new flare of pain and shut my eyes to try to dull it.

Inside the house, mother was talking with Goodie Fisher and Goodie Thatcher – two village wives who had "stopped in" to help her cope with her grief. If they were anything like their daughters, then they weren't being much help.

I'd tried to avoid them, finding a seat on the bench halfway between the house and the shed, built to look out from where the road turned into our walkway to the house. But I hadn't been able to avoid their daughters.

"My mother says that your mother should have had more children," Heldra Thatcher – Goodie Thatcher's daughter – said from nearby. I couldn't see her long brown braids or her coy smile, but I didn't have to. I'd been seeing Heldra for all my seventeen years, and her smug smile never changed. "You're supposed to have nine or ten in case some die or go crazy, or

run off, or are taken by strange magic, or are just plain disap-
pointing."

"Lucky that your mother had twelve then, isn't it?" I said
drily. If Heldra was my child, I'd jump into the river. She was
just like the Shining Folk. Beautiful to look at, but quick to attack.

The funny thing about my new "sight" was that I could still
see the two of them – sort of. But they didn't really look the
same. Edrina Fisher looked even more big-eyed and vulnerable than I remembered, and she flickered in and out of sight
even more than my parents did, disappearing for minutes at a
time as if she wasn't stable enough to be seen. Heldra, on the
other hand, was ghostlike but there all the time and she wasn't
so beautiful here. Hair that was long and luscious in reality
appeared dull and brittle here. And her rounded, lovely face
looked narrow and peaked here when it could be seen at all.
Strangely, it seemed to suit her better.

"Are you really blind now?" Edrina asked with a sigh. She
sighed a lot. And she was so thin and pale in my new "sight"
that I wondered if those sighs might blow her off into the distance.

"I seem to be," I acknowledged. Any fear or grief I was feeling – and by the heavens was there a lot of that! – I was stuffing down as far as I could get it. The last thing I wanted was
pity. Especially from these two. They were Hulanna's friends,
not mine.

The only other blind person in the village was Goodie Hal-
facres and she was nearly eighty. She hadn't gone blind until
last year. But me? I was still just seventeen – just starting out.

What would I do now that I couldn't see? How was I going to hunt? Or start a family? Or keep a house?

None of the boys would even look at me now. Not that I wanted that. Not at all. I was perfectly fine with living with my parents and hunting with my father and tending goats and I didn't need silly things like romance or dancing in moonlight. I wasn't Hulanna.

My heart ached at the thought of her name. I pushed that away, too.

How was I going to convince them all that I wasn't useless now? How was I going to be fierce and independent if I needed them to tell me where everything was? That was the frustrating part. Not the loss – I didn't want to think of the loss – but the part where I was chained now to other people.

"My mother says you'll never find a man now," Heldra said.

"Yes, it's harder when you can't see them," I agreed. "They can hide in plain sight."

Edrina laughed at my joke but then she lowered her voice secretively. "Did you really see one of the Fair Folk?"

Just hearing their name sent a chill through me all over again. They'd taken her. They'd taken my sister, my best friend, my twin. And I'd never see her again. I'd heard my parents whispering all night in their room. They thought I was asleep, but who could sleep with such loss?

"No one's gone into the circle since that girl did when I was just a baby," my father had said. "What was her name?"

"Junan," my mother replied. "Remember her mother? Old Goodie Calver? She was never the same."

"And the girl never came back," my father said with dull finality.

"I should have been watching them," my mother said. Her voice was wracked with guilt ad I flinched at her words. This wasn't her fault, it was mine.

"They're seventeen. You can't watch them like babies forever, Genda."

"I could have prevented it." Her voice broke with a sob.

And I'd tried to block out their shared tears and guilt after that. Because it wasn't my mother or my father's fault. It was mine.

I grabbed a stone from the ground in front of me and tossed it toward what I thought was the shed. Buildings, trees, rocks – things – were harder to see with this new "sight" than people were. They weren't there at all most of the time, and when they were, they were nothing but faint shadows – which made walking nearly impossible. To make matters worse, there were trails everywhere. Glowing trails that were bright or faint. Faint glowing auras. Ghostly things that I *knew* weren't really there but looked like they were.

I was starting to suspect that what I could "see" was another plane. A spiritual realm instead of a physical one.

"My mother says that if your mother raised you right, you never would have been up near the stones at all," Heldra said.

"But Olen goes up to the stones every day," Edrina said.

"Because it's his *job*," Heldra said. "Not because he's a *bad seed*."

"They *were* beautiful," I said abruptly to Edrina. Because I wanted *people* to stop calling Hulanna a bad seed. Because I wanted to shut *people* up who didn't know what they were talking about. "The most beautiful creatures you'd ever seen. And they had rainbow wings like dragonflies. And one of them told Hulanna that he'd dreamed of her and that they were fated mates."

Edrina sighed. "That's so romantic."

Her aura seemed to shiver and blush pink.

"It's made up," Heldra said, tossing her lank hair. "No Fair Folk would pay the Hunter girls any mind. Not when the village is full of girls prettier than them."

She meant herself, of course, and she was very pretty, but that wasn't what I was thinking about. I was seeing someone – actually seeing them! – for the first time since I lost my sight. And it was him – the Fae who had chased me out of the circle. He was bright with color and detail and what I saw was beauty in fine-planed perfection. The world near him seemed to light up like he was holding a lantern, letting me see it, too. He strolled past us as if he did this every day, scooped up one of the goats in his arms, winked at me, and then disappeared into the ghostly trees.

Coldness filled me, searing through to my core at the same time that my mouth went dry as sawdust.

Should I say something? Should I tell someone that I thought I'd just seen a Fae here? They'd think I was crazy.

"Hunter?" Heldra was saying, "Allie Hunter, did you hear me?"

"Hmmm?" I asked.

"You should know that we are determined to remain your friends," Heldra said as I looked after the Fae. He was here. He was walking through our village. If they could steal my sister through the circle, and pick up goats without anyone seeing them, what else could they steal? "We aren't going to shun you just because you're blind now. We will find little jobs for you and maybe take you on a little outing now and then, right Edrina?"

"Yes," Edrina agreed. "My mother says that charity is a comely trait in a woman."

"*My* mother says that common sense is better," I said, but my heart wasn't in it.

"Fat lot of good it did you and Hulanna. Neither of you had the sense you were born with when you went up to those rocks." Heldra's tone was smug.

That Fae was the only thing I'd seen clearly in days. That and whatever was glowing up in the attic. And that meant that I might actually be dependant on girls like Heldra and Edrina for the rest of my life – desperate for their attention and charity to take me out of my loneliness.

Maybe.

But I'd seen that Fae creeping past my home. And Heldra and Edrina hadn't seen that.

"You'll have to tame that tongue," Heldra scolded. "The infirm should be brave, hopeful, positive spirits of light. No one likes a whiner. Or a cynic."

"I'll remember that," I said gravely. No one liked a smug goat, either and yet Heldra was still alive.

"Allie?" my mother called from inside the house. "Allie Hunter, wait there a moment after our guests leave. I want to show you something."

"Your poor mother," Heldra said with feigned sympathy in her tone. "She still thinks you can see."

She clucked her tongue as her mother and Goodie Fisher swept past, picking up the girls in their wake. They walked with the firm assurance of women who still had their daughters.

Women who had come and done their duty to a fallen friend and definitely not taken a little delight in seeing Genda Hunter brought down a peg or two by her daughters' twin disgraces. Was that how they looked in the real world, or only with my new 'sight'?

Strangely, my hearing seemed more acute than ever. And as I waited for my mother, I heard Olen arriving before I would have been able to catch sight of him.

He walked with a limp like he always did. The sound of his left foot dragging just a bit made it distinctive enough to pick him out easily. Add the fact that his father was already talking to mine over by the goat pen and it was definitely Olen who was easing himself down beside me on the bench. He smelled like the bracken of the mountain plains. He smelled like the circle where I'd lost Hulanna.

"We need to talk, Hunter," I heard Olen's father saying. His voice was faint, carrying from the goat pen where my father had just emerged from the forest, a stag slung over his shoulders. He'd gone hunting this morning – like always. It was his job, after all, to hunt for the village, and that didn't stop with the loss of a daughter.

"I'm missing a goat," my father said.

Of course, he was. I'd seen it stolen. Would he believe me if I told him?

"More than goats are missing. And that's only the beginning."

Chapter Four

"How about I guess your secrets, and you only have to tell them to me if I'm right," Olen said softly. He strummed his mandolin quietly, but the noise was enough to drown out my father's conversation. Right when it was getting good. Typical boys. They ruined everything. But you couldn't say, 'Quiet, I'm eavesdropping!' Could you?

I turned to him, surprised at how clear he was to me. My expression must have shown my surprise.

"Let me guess, I look better now that you can't see." He snickered.

But the funny thing was that he did. Olen wasn't much to look at normally. He was taller than most in the village and his muscles hadn't filled out because he was barely older than me. That made him gawky. Especially when you added the limp and the ever-present mandolin.

The last time I'd seen him he had a normal oval-shaped face with the typical blemishes of someone who wasn't fully a man yet. I knew more about them than I wanted to since Goodie Chanter had been by the house to ask mother if she had any cures for bad skin in her grandmother's box in the attic. Grandmother had been a Traveler and Travelers were known for magic cures and tinctures and charms – even if I was pretty sure that was just something they let people believe so that they'd leave them alone.

Travelers aside, I would only have described Olen as pretty average – although he was also my only friend so that made him better than average to me. But he looked different now. Better. The blemishes were gone, for starters. And he radiated a kind of pure light that made everything seem simpler – clearer.

"Well, now you know my secret," I teased. "Guessed it in one."

But I didn't want to poke at him too much. I liked the feeling of simplicity my new "sight" gave me around him. And I liked being visited by Olen.

"Your mom doesn't have any Traveler cures for blindness?" he asked.

"If she does, she's been awfully stingy with them. Is that you still guessing my secrets?"

He cleared his throat. "Here's a guess. It wasn't your idea to go up to the Star Stones."

"Anyone could guess that. Hulanna is the dreamy one, not me. But don't start talking about how Hulanna was a bad seed or blind or not, I'll whack you with this stick!" I felt for the stick. It had been there a minute ago.

"It's four more inches to your right," he said helpfully.

I grabbed the stick. "Right. This stick."

"I'm trembling with fear of your big stick."

I snickered. This was why I liked Olen. Why we sat on the edges of most village gatherings together in happy silence or simple talk. He didn't play games or cause drama. He was just Olen.

"Here's another guess. You saw the ones who took her."

"One," I admitted, my face coloring. "There was one who took her."

"And he was beautiful." Olen sounded like he knew.

"Were you watching from the bushes? I don't remember seeing you there."

"It's called glamor – they have it and they use it. They can make themselves look like the most beautiful creatures on the planet, but in the morning, it's all gone, and you're left with what they really are."

"Kind of like marrying Heldra."

He snorted a laugh. "Oh, Heldra's not so bad."

Of course, he thought that. He was male and she was beautiful. I worked hard not to let a sour expression come over my face.

"How do you know so much about the Shining Ones?" I demanded.

"You know it's my job to play music around town. I'll be Chanter when my father is done."

"Sure. That mandolin is already getting on my nerves."

He picked out a little riff that I was sure was just for me. "You don't think we just play music to entertain the town, do you? That doesn't really sound like a valuable job."

"Well, I didn't want to mention that ..."

"The music keeps them back – the Fair Folk. It blinds them – almost like our own kind of glamor. What my father and I do is like guard work. We're guarding all of you against the Shining Ones. Against the spirit world."

"Well, I'd say that I can see you've done a fine job, only I can't see on account of having not being guarded very well."

His spirit shrugged. "You can't protect people from their own stupidity."

"I guess I deserved that."

But that didn't mean it didn't sting.

"I had a dog once who got a thorn in his paw. He'd always been the most gentle creature."

"Blackie," I said.

"Don't interrupt. He slept in my bed. Ate from my hand. But when he stepped on that thorn, he snapped at everyone until it came out. Bit me and left a mark. I'd show it to you if you could see."

I snapped my reply. "But I can't see. That's worse than a thorn."

"I know." He sounded like he actually meant it. "I just meant to say that I won't take all that snapping personally."

"So, what are you doing here?" He was starting to irritate me with all his understanding and acceptance. It was making it too easy to cry. And I didn't want to cry. "Looking to get bit?"

"I was going to offer you a job."

I barked a laugh. "In case it hasn't been made clear, I'm blind."

"Here's my last guess," he said, and his words were slow, like he was almost worried about this guess. "I want to get Hulanna back. And I think you'll want that, too."

Chapter Five

I swallowed. That was all I wanted – to get her back. That was even more important than my sight. But would she even want to come back? Did I care what she wanted when her choices had already hurt my parents so much? She was an idiot to go.

I felt a little guilty at thinking that.

I'd been there, after all, and I knew it wouldn't be easy to say no to that Shining One when he said she was his fated mate. Maybe she was off in an enchanted world of gemstones and magic and fast-beating wings, enjoying sweet-tasting kisses with that gorgeous winged creature, threading her fingers through his hair and running them over ...

"Allie," my mother said a little breathlessly as she joined us. I could hear the small scuffling sounds of Olen standing up and backing away. He was always shy. He'd be trying to make himself shorter and hide his limp. I knew that look he always had when someone noticed him.

I glanced at him, but in whatever world I was looking at, he was tall and straight, and his smile was confident.

"Goodie Hunter," he said gently as his mandolin quieted. "My deepest condolences on the loss of your daughter. I'll take my leave."

"Chanter," my mother acknowledged, and her voice hitched a little. Maybe she hadn't heard many honest-sounding condolences yet. Chances were pretty good that Heldra's mother was as good at rubbing salt in the wounds as her daughter was. "I thank you for your condolences."

He left to join his father as they set out on the road again. My gaze trailed after them. I wanted to go, too.

Our village – Skundton – was in the shape of a cross with the important things like the inn and tavern, bakery and smithy at the crossroads and everything else moving outward on the four roads according to importance. Edrina and Heldra's parents' shops were close to the center, while our small home and goat pens were at the furthest end of the North Road. There was no one past us – not even farms since the soil turned hard and rocky here and the thorny bushes made clearing anything a nuisance. Only the graveyard lay further north and west.

And yet, Olen and his father were not headed south to town, they took the narrow trail to the north. Would they go to check the Star Stones? Would they play music there like Olen suggested they did?

"Any improvement, Allie?" my mother asked gently.

I turned my head to her, blinking painfully at the way her image flickered in and out of sight. She was holding something bright – so bright that I couldn't make it out easily. I could see her kindly smile through the flickering and blurring and a tear formed in my eye. I blinked it away rapidly.

"Not really," I admitted. "I can make out some blurry things, but ... no. No improvement."

Should I tell her about the Fae I thought I saw? What would they do with me if they thought I was crazy as well as blind?

Would they send me to the healers in the lowlands? The rumors suggested that they were not kind to those who were mentally afflicted.

"Give it time, love," she said, kissing me on the forehead.

"I'm so sorry, mother," I said, trying not to break into sobs as my lips trembled at my admission. "This is all my fault. I should have stopped Hulanna. I should have – "

She cut me off with the press of a finger to my lips. "Hush now, love. There will be no more talk of that. What happened, happened and can't be taken back and we all bear the blame together. Here. I'd almost forgotten that I had this, but I remembered when Goodie Thatcher was going on in my ear about your sight. It was my grandmother's – something that belonged to her people, the Travelers – and it's yours now."

I reached out and took what she handed me It felt sleek and smooth and long. "A scarf?"

"You can't see the pattern, of course, but it's beautifully made of some fine fabric we've no access to here. My grandmother always said that the wearing of it brought second sight." She laughed with chagrin. "A foolish notion, of course, but I don't know. With Fair Folk and magic and loss of sight ... well, maybe the idea of a magical scarf isn't so strange, eh?"

"Thank you, mother," I said, stroking the scarf. It felt beautiful to my touch.

"Given her the magic scarf, have you?" my father asked, joining us. He flickered in and out like a faint ghost of himself and he carried something in his hands. It was so frustrating that objects didn't make more of a mark in this new vision of mine. "Good. Well, I'm off. Stag is hanging in the shed. If you have time, you can deal with it."

"Off?" my mother said, and I could hear the fear and worry in her tone.

"We're not the only ones to see losses today, Genda." His voice was heavy. "We're down a goat. And Crofter has lost a cow. And Fisher says he lost two big fish right out of his smoker."

"What does that have to do with you?" my mother asked. "We just lost a child! You need to stay and grieve with me, Hunter."

"And the Earthmover family lost their baby. Just two years old, she is. Gone."

My mother gasped and I felt like the air had been sucked out of me, too.

"Their baby?" I asked in a small voice. "But a baby couldn't get up to the Star Stones on her own."

"The poor little mite," my mother said grimly. "The poor, poor little darling. It's the old things come back. In my mother's day, you kept your kiddies close and nailed horseshoes on the door and left out milk for the Fair Folk."

"That sounds crazy. What could milk do to protect anyone?" I scoffed. I'd seen the Shining Ones. I didn't think they'd be too impressed with saucers of milk.

"More than one baby was carried off in those days. Stolen by the Shining Ones. But I still don't know what that has to do with you, Hunter."

"I'm Hunter for this village, Genda," my father said grimly. "And I must push my grief aside and do my duty. I can hunt anything and bring it down. There's a price to that.

"You know I found that Ice Bear last year after he killed old Crabtree. Took me four days in a blizzard, but I brought him down. When you're Hunter for the village, you hunt what the village needs hunted, be that meat or be that threat. That's the price."

"But alone? It's too dangerous!" I could hear the fear in my mother's voice. She'd just lost a daughter. She couldn't bear to lose a husband now, too. And yet, he was right. We were the Hunters for our village, and I had been chosen by lot to follow my father in the responsibility. If honor and duty meant anything, then it meant doing the jobs that had to be done even when they were too big for you to do.

I cleared my throat. "I'm coming, too, father."

Chapter Six

"Absolutely not." My father's voice was as hard as the rock under our feet. "This is dangerous. And you are blind."

I gritted my teeth. "I can hunt blind. This is my fault, Father. I went with Hulanna up to the Star Stone ring. And when she went in ... something came out."

"You saw it?" His tone changed. Now he was all business. A hunter looking for sign.

"It chased me, and I ran into one of the standing stones. That's when I lost my sight."

My mother made a sad sound in the back of her throat, but my father was still intent on the details.

"What kind of a creature did you see?"

"He looked like a man, but he was thinner and more beautiful with perfect features," I said. "He had wings, but he wasn't flying."

My father's tone was considering. "Did he wear boots or shoes?"

I tried to think back. I hadn't been looking at his feet, had I?

"I don't know. But I'm pretty sure that I saw him steal our goat."

"You're blind, girl," he said, and his tone was almost harsh – but it wasn't harsh with me, but more harsh *for* me – like he wanted to shove that aside as badly as I did.

"I see some things," I protested. "I can't explain it. Some glimmers of people – but they look different than they do for real. I saw the Shining One who chased me stealing our goat. I can see this scarf that Mother gave me. I see some things."

"Second sight," my mother said with wonder in her voice. "She lost her first sight, but she still has second sight – the ability to see things on another plane. A different dimension than ours."

"Plane?" my father's tone was as cynical as mine would have been a few days ago. "Dimension? That's all nonsense. Magical nonsense."

"It wasn't nonsense to my mother or her mother."

"Because they were crazy. Travelers. Magic lovers. Crazy people. You know I love you, Genda, but you come from a line of dreamers and fools."

"Well, explain what she's seeing then," my mother said, boldness in her tone.

"She's seeing what she wants to see. Imaginings. Wishes."

"I didn't wish the goat away," I said firmly, crossing my arms. "And I'm coming with you. After all, I am a Hunter, too. If this is your responsibility, then it's mine, too."

My father sighed. "If you come, you'll have to keep up. And you'll have to do it on your own. I have a predator to track and hunt and no time to lead you around."

"She can't!" my mother began, but my father cut her off.

"Do you think you can manage to follow me by sound and this imaginary sight of yours?"

"Yes," I said bravely. Of course, he didn't believe me. I wouldn't believe me, either.

"Well. Alright then," he said. He kissed me roughly on the forehead. "Bravery is a good thing to have. Now, kiss your mother while I find you a staff. We have ground to cover and daylight is wasting."

Chapter Seven

The staff, it turned out, was a good idea. I grabbed it tightly as I tripped – again! – over a root I couldn't see. Trees had shadows in this world – ghostly, faint things that glowed green, but they seemed to move and twist whenever I looked right at them crossing my eyes and giving me a headache and that made watching for their roots nearly impossible. Fortunately, I could follow my father's bright glow ahead of me.

"Stay five paces or more behind," he'd said. "I'll keep an eye out for you, but I want to spread out. We'll see more that way. Tell me if you see any sign of the little girl or those Fair Folk. We're going to get these Shining rats."

We were more alike than most people realized. I wanted to get the Shining rats, too. And then I wanted to see them hang in my father's shed like that stag.

I didn't see signs of the Fair Folk. What I mostly saw were strange things. The ghostly trees were ringed by tiny stars in drifts like snowflakes in winter. Little trails of smoke-like color swirled up from the trail or around the trees in almost indiscernible clouds. My familiar woods of velvet shadows and warm autumn light had transformed into a dark fairyland where stars replaced autumn leaves and strange glowing strands replaced hard-packed dirt trails.

Other trails wove through the ghost trees in colored ribbons– red or purple or gold. I was sure they each led somewhere, and I felt the urge to follow them, almost as if I was being drawn to the ribbons. Had they always been here in the woods and high mountain plains near our village or were they new things? Someone ought to follow them and find out where they led. Just not today. Not with the Earthmover baby missing.

Movement flickered just outside my line of sight.

What was that?

I took another step toward my father, feeling outward with the staff. I was sure I'd seen something. If only I was carrying a bow like he was! Not that it would be very safe with my vision the way it was, but I'd *feel* safer.

There it was again. So fast that I could barely see it at all.

I swallowed, choking down fear. I wasn't sure if I was ready to face them again. I could almost feel the brush of fingers on my back like I had when he was chasing me from the Star Stone circle.

"Father?" I called quietly. He wouldn't want me calling too loudly. Not on a hunt. Even this might be too loud.

Nothing.

Another movement in the trees.

And then he stepped forward. Not my father. *Him.*

I could see him clearly – unlike the shadowy world around us.

His unearthly beauty marked him as Fae, though not the Fae who had chased me out of the circle – unless they could change how they looked. Huge wings almost half again as tall as he was – black swirling woodsmoke – shot out from his shoulders and his long raven hair swirled around sharp, pointed features and delicate ears. He was utterly beautiful. Non-human. Otherworldly. Heart-meltingly gorgeous. Everything about him screamed to me, *You aren't worthy, mortal. I will take what I want from you because you never deserved to have it in the first place.*

He smiled slightly, tilting his head to the side with a glitter in his gorgeous black eyes. He gathered his hair up between his fingers and tied it back into a tight knot.

"Want to play, mortal girl?" he asked.

I could just imagine what kind of games this Fae would want to play – they probably involved taking things from me one by one.

"Oh look, you said my name in your head, mortal," he said with an eager smile. "'*Fae.*' Don't you know that calls me? It opens your mind to me. Do you want me to read your thoughts, little mortal?"

I tried to think of him as small and weak. Tried hard to project the idea of me being invulnerable and strong while he was nothing to me. Nothing. Nothing.

"Oh, that's cute, little mortal." He laughed and for a moment his image flickered. For just a half-second I saw him as a feral creature. A red gleam tinged those beautiful green eyes. His clothing wasn't finely tailored trousers and boots and coat. They were rags and bones and feathers. And those wings were nothing but bone with scraps of skin hanging from them, like when a stag sheds his velvet. His teeth were pointed like wolves' and his face was far too narrow to be beautiful and around him, there was some sense that even now I wasn't really seeing him as he was. That something even darker and more twisted lay beneath this second surface.

And then it was like an iron curtain slammed over my view and his beauty was back – maybe even more intensely than before. It left me breathless.

I would do anything for him. Anything at all. Deny my family. Flee my sense of self. Give him everything. He was *worth* everything. I'd give all I had, all I was, for him, for him. My heart felt like it was dancing.

I stepped forward, my heart soaring forward with me, pushing me further at the thought of him, just wanting to be closer, just wanting to feel that glow for another moment.

His smile deepened.

"That's better," he said.

Musical strains of a mandolin – faint, but there – tickled the edges of my hearing.

"In the moonlight…" the faint song being sung tickled the edges of my hearing *"… in the noonday …"*

The Shining One frowned. I was careful not to even think the other word anymore. Why was I being careful not to think it? When I wanted nothing more than to give him my whole mind? My whole self …

The mandolin was growing louder. And now I could hear it was Olen singing.

"Noonlight, Moonlight, Noonday moonlight!"

It was ridiculous. A folk song that didn't even make sense. And yet the glorious being in front of me stood still, eyes glazed over as if he was stunned by the ridiculous folk tune. As if it captivated him like he captivated me.

"Allie?" Olen called. He paused his playing as he asked, "Why are you just standing there? Allie Hunter?"

As if the spell was broken, the Shining One winked at me and then crouched, bunching his wings, before leaping into the air, wings spread out and gliding away through the ghastly branches of the trees.

I let out a long breath. He'd almost had me. He'd almost seduced me from reason like Hulanna had been seduced.

"Olen?" I croaked through a dry throat.

"We found the Earthmover baby, Allie. There's no threat after all."

But there was a threat. And I'd just seen it. It had almost stolen my soul.

Chapter Eight

"At least she's safe," my mother said that evening when we returned. "It was a false alarm."

"She must have wandered off," my father said, but his voice was still cautious. It wasn't like him to jump to conclusions and it was still very strange to find a baby out in the woods safe, alive, unhurt. Especially so far from home.

I hadn't told him about the Shining One I saw. I felt the knowledge of it burning in my chest – a secret wanting to get out and spread from person to person. And yet. They already didn't trust me because of Hulanna. I'd heard Chanter whispering to my father that he should keep an eye on me. And when I'd asked Olen if he'd seen the Shining One, he'd laughed and said that only I would have the audacity to claim to see the Fair Folk when I couldn't see at all.

If I told them that I'd seen one – again – and a different one than before, would they even believe me? They'd want to know why I hadn't called for help. And how would I explain that delightful, toxic, enchanting tangle of emotions I'd felt at the sight of him? My cheeks were hot even now at the thought of it.

"Even so, perhaps we should find some of the old artifacts," my mother mused. "The things our grandmothers hid for use someday when *they* returned."

She said 'they' like she was afraid to even use the words Shining Ones or Fair Folk instead of 'Fae.' Did she know that saying their name in your mind called them?

"Old wives' tales," my father scoffed. "They weren't true then and they aren't true now."

"They wouldn't have gone to all the trouble of hiding artifacts if they weren't true," my mother chided. "The Iron Ring, the Nail Pendant, the Cage of Souls ..."

"Genda," my father's voice was gentle. "You look to these things because you're blinded by grief. Mourn with me, instead. We have some time now."

I heard a rustling of cloth and their glowing forms merged – a hug perhaps. It was hard to tell with my new vision. I closed my eyes, grateful for the rest from the headache-inducing images of my second sight – or whatever it was.

"I'm going to sit in the garden," I said roughly. I was tired. We'd walked a long way before the Earthmover girl was found.

"Sit with us," my mother offered, but sadness was thick in her voice and I knew tears were close. My parents could cry together. Tears were the last thing I wanted right now. Tears would mean defeat and I wasn't willing to give up yet. There had to be a way to bring her back.

"I just need some time on my own," I said, using the staff to help me find my way to the door.

The night air, cool on my face, was alive with the scents of flowers going to sleep and the sound of goats as they settled for sleep. Someone needed to walk them up to pasture. They'd been left in the pen all day and that would make them cranky. But that was my job. Mine and Hulanna's and Hulanna was gone.

What I needed was some kind of advantage. I already had a disadvantage – losing my sight – and I didn't call this new strange sight a proper exchange for that. So, what I needed was some tool to get my edge back. Maybe, if I found one of these ancient things my mother was talking about, I could even things out again.

But how did you find ancient artifacts? My mother didn't seem to be too clear on that.

It seemed like just the kind of thing old ladies would do, too. Where should we put emergency artifacts for future generations? Oh, I don't know, let's hide them so they're really difficult to find when they're needed again. That way, if someone finds them, we'll know that they're worthy. But what if someone just stumbles on them in their secret hiding space? Well, then *that* person is worthy. Unworthy people don't find magical artifacts in the woods, right?

I sat down on our garden bench and thought about it, letting my second sight wander over the bright flowers – somehow their flower souls were almost more lovely than their real blossoms were – and the ribbons of color that wove through the landscape. They called to me again. Especially the golden one that seemed to pulse with light whenever I looked at it.

I was just sure that it would lead me to something incredible. Listen to me! I was as crazy as those ancestor women.

I bit my lip glancing at our cottage. My mother's sobs were easy to hear, and I was pretty certain that my father would be tearful, too. No point bothering them. No point bothering anyone on a mere hunch.

I could do this myself, couldn't I? I wasn't useless just because I'd lost my sight. I clenched my jaw forcing away thoughts of blindness. I'd deal with all those emotions later – when the threat was past. When everyone was safe. This was my fault and I would fix it and if these ribbons of color could lead me to some clue to help out, then I'd be a fool not to follow them. Right?

So, why did it take so much work to talk myself into it?

I pushed that thought aside, grabbed my staff and carefully worked my way to the golden ribbon. It almost seemed to greet me as it pulsed brighter at my arrival. I'd made it! But which way now?

I looked up and down the ribbon, but it wasn't clear which way to go to follow it. Well, I'd just have to guess. One end curled toward town – not ideal. Not when I was navigating with a staff and anyone else could see me slinking around.

I'd go the other way and just hope I'd chosen correctly.

Perhaps by chance, or perhaps by fate, the ribbon led along a well-worn path winding toward the east of Skundton. My feet were quiet on the packed earth and I was navigated as much by memory as by the golden ribbon, letting the staff swing back and forth in front of me as I walked so I didn't slam a toe into a root or rock.

My eyes drifted painfully over the ever-changing ghostly landscape. Trees flickered in and out of life at random. Stars and bright murals of light sprang to life and then faded, leaving only whispers behind them. It made me nauseated.

It was in that silence that I heard whispering. Someone did not know I was here.

"If they really are back, then it's *her* fault. I'm telling you, Olen, you shouldn't be around that girl."

I felt my cheeks heat. Whoever that was whispering in the forest had to be talking about me. The voice was familiar, but I didn't dare look around the trees to place it for sure. The only thing worse than having people talk about you behind your back was letting them know you knew that they all thought you were pathetic.

"She's blind. What do you expect me to do, treat her poorly after she lost her sight? Be reasonable."

"I just don't think that if you're serious about *us*, that you should be around her."

Ha! Olen had a girlfriend. And she didn't like me.

Well, I had bigger things to worry about than boys. She could have that mandolin-loving Chanter for all I cared. And they could spend all their time together talking about me and my blindness if that's what they thought was so entertaining. I had a sister to save, an artifact to find, and a new world to navigate. My decision on that wasn't going to be shaken by a gawky teen who played obnoxious music on his aged mandolin.

So why did their words sting so much?

Chapter Nine

By the time I began to regret my decision, it was already too late.

It was growing colder. Cold enough that I had to assume that the sun had set long ago. I'd already stumbled and fallen so many times that I'd lost count. The chances that my soft woolen hose were torn were almost certain, but I didn't dare to stop to find any holes or tend painful knees. If I didn't prove this had all been worth something before I returned home, I'd have nothing to show for this trip but my parent's grief and disappointment. If I could find whatever was at the end of this ribbon – well, I'd have that, right?

It was strange, but the ribbon almost seemed to whisper to me, as if I could hear the voice of the person who had originally made this trail.

Hide it. Hide it somewhere safe for when they come back.

Which had to mean that I was on the right path! If I could bring something back that was valuable, then I'd show them that I could still be the village Hunter. Somehow.

Blindness was only a ... situation ... not a sentence.

There was a shuffle ahead and a pink-tinted streak zipped across the path with a ribbon trail of its own, though the colors faded almost immediately. I'd just barely caught sight of a pair of long pointy ears. Rabbit.

See? I could still see animals. A bit. I could see their spirits. That had to be something I could use to hunt, right?

A branch thwapped me in the face and I bit back a cry of pain. It had hit me right in the eyes. I closed them – sinking into darkness as even my second sight left me – and tried not to cry in pain and frustration.

Who was I kidding? Stumbling blindly through the forest wasn't going to do anything, was it?

Trap their souls. Send them back. Keep us safe. On the track.

Whoever left that golden ribbon must have also been fond of bad poetry.

Gritting my teeth together, I opened my painful eyes and pressed on. I'd come this far. I could keep going. I just hoped I was back before my parents got too worried.

The path twisted around the corner of a rocky outcrop – or that's what it seemed to be when it tapped it with my staff – and I stepped up onto a rocky shelf, following the ribbon carefully. Shale slipped under my feet and I scrambled to keep upright. I must be somewhere steep. I tapped the rock with my staff, but it seemed solid ahead.

When I looked up, I saw it.

A magnificent stag, glowing light blue in the darkness ahead, stood looking up at the sky, his antlers sweeping wide behind him. Beautiful. Unlike the rabbit, his ghost stayed bright, stomping a foot and pawing the ground with a snort.

As a Hunter, I should be excited to see a strong animal like that so close to our village. And of course, I was. But mostly I was just in awe. Who would have thought that blindness could lead to a sight like this? I blinked my aching eyes and stayed very still until he ducked his head and slipped around something up ahead.

The ribbon led to the very place he'd stood, and I followed it the moment he disappeared, sliding and skidding uphill over the loose slate. A tumbling sound followed by a clatter worried me. Was I higher than I thought I was?

Night breezes blew around me, whipping up my light shirt and short jacket. I needed to dress warmer. The woolly collar around my neck wasn't going to be enough to keep me warm if the night grew much cooler.

Find it, find it, find it.

Whoever had left this ribbon trail must have been single-minded about her purpose. That voice that echoed through the spiritual trail she'd left was loud and strong.

The ribbon trail took a sharp turn and I followed, smacking my forehead into a rocky ledge. I bit back a curse. I needed to check both the ground and the air with my staff if I didn't want to do that again. I rubbed my forehead, fighting against the sharp pain.

I was still seeing stars as I tapped out a clear space with the staff. I was heading into a cave. Not a good idea when I didn't have any idea where it led.

It felt even colder within the rocks – as if winter hid in this cave while it was autumn outside. I worked my way slowly, tapping, tapping, tapping. It had better not drop off in here! If it did and I didn't notice, I could fall to my death. I'd heard of that happening to people in caves. It was why you were always supposed to bring a light with you – though a light wouldn't do much of anything for me right now.

Loose rock in thick piles skidded under my soft boots. Had someone dug this cave with a pick, or was it naturally formed?

And should I be worried about bears or other big creatures who preferred caves for shelter?

The golden trail took a sudden turn upward and I felt up with my hands, careful to keep my head low. No hitting it on the rock this time, thank you!

There was a ledge in the rock above me. You wouldn't be able to see it from the entrance, but it was thick and strong. I carefully twisted my body so I could reach my hands into the rocky shelf.

The trail ended here.

I held my breath as I reached. There! Something cold and metal to the touch! I dragged it out from the ledge and clasped it to my chest.

I'd found something!

I felt it carefully. Was it a cage? It was the length of my fore-arm – maybe a little shorter and taller than it was fat with a handle at the top and woven wire around the outside and a sol-id metal bottom. Yes. A small cage like you might keep a bird in – if you were cruel enough to trap a bird and keep it from the sky.

As I touched it, it sprang to life, glowing an eerie bluish-green. I felt drawn to it and repelled at the same time.

I'd found something! Could this be the Cage of Souls my mother had talked about?

I couldn't wait to show her. With a smile, I turned around to leave the cave and the breath wooshed out of my lungs.

The golden ribbon was gone.

Chapter Ten

No, no, no! My thoughts were foggy and lightning fast as I tried to manage my spiking emotions.

What was I going to do? How was I going to get home without my ribbon to guide me? I scrambled out of the cave, my staff tapping to find the entrance.

My breath was too rapid, making thought even harder. I was worse than lost. I was blind and lost. And I'd been so confident just a minute ago! I bit my lip.

There it was! The entrance.

I collapsed onto the ground in relief. At least I wasn't lost wandering underground. I just needed a minute to sit, staff in one hand and cage in the other. I took tally of where I was, trying to be logical about it and not let screeching anxiety block out thought.

The air was cold – so it was still night, then. I had no easy way back home – in fact, without the ribbon or the ability to identify landmarks, I was pretty much lost. And since I'd never been here before, it was safe to say that other people from the village weren't out here picnicking or collecting berries. I wouldn't be able to call for help.

At least I was physically well, except for being blind and my eyes stinging from where the branches struck them.

I wanted to cry.

But brave girls who just found ancient artifacts that might save everyone don't cry, right? I sniffed back tears, wiping my eyes with the back of my hand and then wiping it on my short coat and jerkin. No tears. At least I had my belt knife and tinder – for all the use they would be.

I tried to think about strengths I had. I could see any Shining Ones who came creeping around – that was more than most people could see. I should be grateful for that. I could have been left with *no* sight instead of at least having second sight.

Yes, that was an advantage. I took a long, settling breath letting my single advantage remind me that I wasn't helpless and that meant I wasn't hopeless either.

But my eyes still stung. I needed a way to protect them. I couldn't close them, or I'd lose even the little bit of help from second-sight that I had. Would I still have that if they were covered – maybe loosely?

I dug into my pocket and pulled out the scarf my mother had given me. It still glowed bright – a swirl of colors and beauty. With care, I folded it into a long slender roll – not too thick, but enough to provide some protection. Hopefully, I could wrap this around my eyes light enough to keep them open but tight enough to protect them from scratching branches. I brought it up, tying it tightly around the back of my head.

Color filled my vision.

I gasped.

My sight was back. What ...? How ...?

I was sitting on a rocky ledge – sharp in shadow and gilding light. The first rays of dawn spread over the rippling landscape like pouring honey over a cake. The golden light bathed the hills and filled up the runnels, pouring ever outward as it flowed from east to west.

I could see so far from here beyond where the road out of town became a twisting path as it shot toward the kingdoms below and out to the sea.

My heart lurched at how high up I was, but the temporary stab of fear was nothing compared to the wonder of seeing again.

Was I ... healed? Maybe father had been wrong all along and the Travelers had magical abilities woven into their articles. This scarf had done something to me. Did I dare to believe it had healed me?

The golden half-light of early morning was so beautiful that tears sprang up in my eyes. Warmth and gratitude spread over me. Even if it didn't last, even if I just had it for now – oh, it was beautiful!

Down the mountainside and to the west, Skundton could be seen – a cluster of smoke trails winding up to the sky in a little clearing.

My parents would be waking there. Hopefully, only now noticing that I was gone. Or better yet, assuming I was out in the village already.

And I would be able to bring them this cage.

I lifted it up to inspect it and gasped. It was nothing but a rusty old birdcage. It had none of the power I'd felt in the cage or seen with my second sight. The teal glow was gone.

What had happened? I scrambled back into the cave. Maybe it only worked here. But it still looked dull and useless in the cave. I'd ruined it somehow. It was worthless now.

With a sigh, I went back out into the sun and held it up, disappointment thick in my heart. I'd failed at this, too.

Or had I? Perhaps this magical gift – this scarf that brought back sight – perhaps it changed how I saw the cage.

Curious, I slipped the blindfold off and the world went black. Only the cage burned bright in front of me, glowing with eerie blue-green light. Magical swirling letters rimmed the top and base of the cage, flowing into one another in a way that was unreadable but beautiful. I tried to pick them out, squinting but it only gave me a headache. I couldn't shake the overwhelming feeling that this was a powerful weapon of my grandmothers before me.

Wow!

I looked up, but the world was dark again, only faint glowing shadows and flickering stars of light remained. The golden dawn had disappeared. I swallowed disappointment down. The scarf hadn't healed me at all.

Experimentally, I slipped the blindfold back on. Bright light crashed into my mind, sending a stab of pain and joy through my head.

I could see again! I sighed with relief.

So, I'd have to wear the scarf all the time. That was okay. It was better than losing my sight again. I tried not to let the disappointment at not really being healed from filling me. There was no point mourning what never was. This was simply the way things were now. Whining about it would get me nowhere. Heldra had been right about that part.

When I looked at the cage again, it was nothing but a rusty old piece of junk.

They didn't even need to hide it. It was hiding in plain sight.

But now something else occurred to me – as magical as this scarf was and as amazing as it was that it returned my sight to me – did it block my second-sight? As long as I was wearing it, I wouldn't see the spiritual plane, would I? I wouldn't see what was going on that no one else could see.

I had my sight back, but I'd lost something in return. I couldn't find my way home without it, but I also couldn't see the Fae slipping through the woods with it on.

What an interesting predicament.

I clambered down the steep shale path, leaning on the staff, even though I could see. Shale bounced down the path and dropped down the steep edge into the trees far below.

I'd climbed this in the dark. I was crazy. I probably should have died climbing this last night. And yet, I couldn't help the joy soaring in my heart. I could hunt again! I could see people! And I had a cage that did ... something.

Now, if I could just find a way to harness all this, maybe I could cross that circle of stones myself and bring back my sister.

I'm coming for you, Hulanna. Hold on.

Chapter Eleven

When you know you're blind to something, you feel like you can sense it everywhere. At every bend in the path, around every corner, behind every tree, I thought I could see Fae. Shining Ones. I had to remember not to say their name, or I'd lose the privacy in my own mind.

But if they could control me by making me think a certain way, hadn't I already lost to them? I slipped my blindfold off and scanned around me – only to find nothing at all out of the normal – so many times that I'd lost count. I needed to calm down and stop jumping at every shadow. I'd hunted predators with my father before. Calm was key.

Even with my sight, the path home wasn't clear. As soon as I was down from the mountain trail, the dense growth blocked any real landmarks. The path I'd traveled last night had disappeared as if it never was. I was pushing west by the sun – but was I angled south enough to reach the village? If I angled south too far, I should reach the rushing Mattervine River. I should know this part of the forest. It should be easy to find my way, but I hadn't ventured off the known paths before – not very far at least, and every clump of trees and raspberry-cane-infested patch of glen was beginning to look the same.

Fear filled me at the thought of being lost out here with the Fae loose. I refused to let it control me, though, turning it to determined anger in my mind. So, they thought they could scare me and control me, did they? I would show them that I was no easy prey.

A storm was brewing in the woods. The winds so strong that they blew away any woodland sounds that might help guide me.

Calm, Hunter, Calm.

By the time I stumbled from the forest to the brushy mountain plain, I was winded, thirsty, and tired. The rocky plain rolled out in front of me, a tumble of broken rock chunks, lichen, and tangled low bushes.

"Allie! Oh, thank goodness, it's you!" Olen scrambled up from a lichen-covered rock he was sitting on. In the high winds, I hadn't even heard his mandolin.

I'd veered too far north and ended up emerging in the rocky mountain plains where the Star Stones guarded the entrance to the Faewald. Regret ripped at me more strongly than the raging wind as I stole a look at it. It seemed so unbearably simple. Just a ring of stones.

A ring of stones my sister had disappeared into. A ring that had ruined my life.

And here was Olen, looking a bit jumpy, his eyes going everywhere at once. But he was just plain Olen with his oval face and blemished skin and nervous stoop as he tried not to look too tall. He limped over to me and tugged on my long red braid awkwardly.

"Should have seen you a mile away with that red hair, Allie. You stand out in the woods like a cardinal up from the valley. But I thought you were a ghost."

I knew not to judge him by looks anymore. Though I could live without the comments on my hair. I knew how he looked on the other plane and that tempered how I saw him here.

On a whim, I pulled my blindfold off so I could see him properly. He flashed to life the moment it passed my eyes. He was bright glowing blue and other vibrant colors as his spirit self took over – wavering and smudged but also beautiful. That oval face looked stronger now – there was something about the set of the jaw that made him look more powerful and more de-termined. He was suddenly straight and tall, his head held so high that I wouldn't have laughed if someone put a crown on it. He vibrated with music. As if it was as much a part of him as his own flesh. I sighed with relief.

"I went out into the woods last night to find an old arti-fact," I said as an explanation, but I wasn't able to say more as my gaze drifted past him toward the Star Stones.

"Have you lost your mind, Allie Hunter?" Was he mad? His eyes flashed. What did he have to be angry about? "Do you know why I thought you were a ghost? Your father was worried sick! He went after you. He and my dad set me to watch while they were gone."

Anxiety filled his voice, but it was nothing compared to what I was feeling with my blindfold off.

The Star Stone circle was *full* of Shining Ones. They filled every inch of the space available, pushing against the edges of the circle as if there was a barrier there that no one could feel but them.

Their eyes were hungry and their jaws tense. So hungry and tense that it almost amplified their striking physical beauty. Male and female, short and tall, dark and fair, they were all shockingly gorgeous with delicate, sweeping wings and clothing that flickered between rags and bones and feathers or magnificent finely cut silks and brocades. Some of them had horns and others tails like foxes or cougars. And all of them had sharp teeth. It was as if their glamor was flickering in and out again and I was seeing them both as the glorious creatures they wanted to be seen as, and the almost feral creatures of reality.

Going into the circle and out of the circle, colored ribbon tracks wove – each of them bright and pulsing as if many important journeys had been made into that circle.

One of them – dark green and so fresh that it seemed more real than the others – called to me. I felt, without knowing how I felt it, that it was somehow connected to my father.

"Allie? Are you listening to me?" Olen sounded panicked. "You're not in there and they went in looking for you!"

"Went in?"

"They went in the circle, Allie! Your dad and mine! They went looking for you and your sister."

No wonder he was angry.

I looked the nearest Fae in the eyes. What had they done with Father when he went in there? And had something else come out? How many of them were out now? One had come out for Hulanna – the one who chased me and stole my goat. But a second Fae had been in the woods with the smoky wings. And now there could be two more – one for Father and one for Chanter.

I pulled my blindfold back on. I needed to not see *them* while I spoke to him. It was too hard seeing their eager looks as he spoke – as if they were sure that they could suck us into their circle, too.

"But I'm not in there," I said as if I could argue sense into them after they'd already acted. My normal vision returned and the circle became a boring ring of stones again and Olen became just a slightly hunched teenager with an anxious expression and nervous fingers that played with the strap of his mandolin as he spoke. "I'm right here. I've never been in there."

"How were they supposed to know that?" he demanded, angry now. "How were they supposed to know when you went missing, too? It was all they could do to keep your mother from leaping into that circle. They didn't let me go. They left me to watch and to play. I've been playing all night, but I haven't seen any Shining Ones. I've just been playin' and fearin' all night since they disappeared."

"All night?" I repeated. Those hungry eyes. Those crowds of Fae. Had they been there when my father went in? Or did they come later? After they had finished whatever they'd done to him. A chill filled me.

Olen grabbed me by the shoulders, shaking me with fear and worry in his eyes. "You aren't listening to me, Allie! Our fathers went in there – past the ring. They were looking for you and your sister. And Allie, no one ever comes out again once they go in. We're Chanter and Hunter now. You and me. Do you get that? There is no one else left to be that but us. And your dad told me you saw a Fae – "his voice stuttered over the word. "Fair Folk loose here in the woods. And my dad said that I have to stay here day and night and play the mandolin to hold them back as much as I can because it's all we have left to keep them out of our world. Don't you understand?"

"Don't say their name," I gasped. "They can hear it in your mind."

"Fae. Fae. Fae," he said, spitting the name as if it didn't matter to him at all. "Who cares if they hear? We're all dead already! That's what *my* mother says. She says I shouldn't bother to stay. All the whispers old wives tell to young wives say the same thing. If anyone goes in the circle, something comes out. One for one. And if even *one* of them gets out, they will destroy us all."

Chapter Twelve

"There are three of them out there somewhere, Allie. Three of them. And both our fathers are in there looking for someone who isn't even there!"

My teeth were chattering – was that from the pressure of all of this happening, or was it from seeing all those ... Shining Ones ... waiting on the other side? I hadn't meant to let them chatter. But I hadn't meant any of this to happen either. I hadn't meant to let my sister go in the circle, I hadn't meant to push my father or Olen's father into going after us. Everything had just spiraled out of control.

Fear – powerful as a winter storm threatened to overwhelm me. My life – everything about it – was gone now. With effort, I shoved the fear away, forcing it to feed my determination instead. I would not let this ruin everything. I wouldn't.

"We need to go in after them, too," I said between my chattering teeth. My blindfold had fallen a little and over the edge of it, I could see the Fair Folk grinning from inside the circle. With every word I said that made it more likely that I might go in there, they seemed more excited. Some were even standing on tip-toe as if to reach for something just beyond their grasp. "We can't leave them in there looking for me when I'm not even there."

Olen made an angry sound in the back of his throat. "It's like you don't even get it."

But I got it. That was the problem. I knew *exactly* what he was telling me. I'd doomed his father and mine to death. And with them, the whole village.

Not fear, Allie – determination. Don't let this stop you. Make it drive you!

"I get it," I forced between gritted teeth. "I've doomed them to die because of me. Because of one decision!"

Olen let out a long breath and looked at me as if he was bringing all the patience he had left to bear on me. My head ached as my two eyes saw him differently – one seeing the hero in the spirit plane and the other seeing the average teen boy.

"Allie." He said each word carefully as if I'd lost my mind along with normal sight. "You. And. I. Are. All. That's. Left."

"I understand," I said. He was still holding my arms as if I was a child he was scolding – or maybe protecting.

"You *don't* understand. We can't go after them, Allie, be-cause you and I are Chanter and Hunter now. I have to stay here day and night and chant and play to keep our enemies at bay and you, Allie. Blind or not – though you can't be all that blind if you went on an adventure in the woods last night, hm-mm? – you must hunt and kill the Fae that are in our woods before they steal our children and livestock and destroy our worlds."

"Worlds?" I asked, and this time I felt stupid. I was pretty sure that there was just one world.

"Each person lives in their own little world with their own little suns that make it alive. For your parents, those suns were called Alastra and Hulanna. What happened to them when they lost their suns, hmmm?"

"Their world ended," I agreed. Mine had ended when I lost Hulanna and my father.

"Yes. So – go save us all before more worlds end, hmm? Can you do that."

I nodded numbly.

He laughed. "I asked that as if it's actually possible. Of course, you're going to fail. I'm going to fail. But we still have to try."

"Has anyone ever told you that you're terrible with people?" I asked.

"Well, I'd been wondering why none of the girls was sweet on me," he said with a rueful smile. "Maybe that's it."

"It's definitely it," I said sharply, though I knew it wasn't true. I'd heard him whispering with one in the woods. The very one who thought I was trouble. It stung that he thought I was stupid and bound to fail and it reminded me that she'd warned him to stay away from me.

Although, if I was being objective, what chance did a blind girl have against magical creatures from another world? Not much. Maybe I was trouble.

"You'd better get back to playing that mandolin if you want to keep people from dying and all that stuff."

He snickered, but he was calming down, at least. "Yes, one mandolin will definitely defeat the hordes. Just don't forget the rhyme, okay? *Music to bind, Fire to blind, Look in their eye, With Iron they die.*"

"I thought that was just a nursery rhyme," I said.

"Our lives are nursery rhymes and Faewald stories, now, Allie. We need to ask some children to help us remember them. Because if we don't, we're going to all die."

"Don't be so dramatic," I said, but my heart wasn't in it. After all, I'd already lost my father and sister. My mother was all that was left. Wasn't that close enough to everyone dying? "I've heard every Faerie story there is. And I plan on ruining them all."

Chapter Thirteen

I was six the first time I sat with my father for deer. It had been a hard winter. Back in town, people were grinding potatoes for flour and rationing each dried bean. Every scrap of meat brought to the town could help.

He'd come in the door with a flurry of snowflakes like glittering stars swirling around him as his breath still plumed in the cold air rushing into our house.

"Come on girls, let's hunt!"

"You shouldn't bring the girls, Hunter," my mother had chided. "They'll only hold you up and we need the meat."

But one look at my big pleading eyes and he'd winked. "Can you be quiet, Allie? Can you be still?"

I had nodded, excitement brimming up inside me. I wanted to be just like my father. Fearless. Unstoppable.

"I'd rather stay by the fire," Hulanna had said and he'd tramped snow across mother's clean floors to join her by the fire and kiss her tumbled curls.

"Stay here, then, poppet."

But he'd taken my little hand in its rabbit mitten with his big one and I'd followed him through the snow, walking in his big footprints.

Around us, the winter ghouls howled in the wind and the trees cracked and moaned, but I was safe with my father and his ash bow.

I was safe even when the ghouls howled close to our hidden winter blind – so close that my knees trembled and twice my father caught my eye with an encouraging smile.

I was safe as they rattled the tree above us.

I was safe as Father leaned in and whispered to me, "Don't let fear drown you. Let it fuel you. Let it make you strong and fiery."

I'd let it burn inside me until my anger at my own fear burned every last scrap of it away and underneath was nothing but bravery.

When the stag finally walked past our blind, there was nothing left in me but determination and fire. Even when we had to drag the deer through the snow with ghouls howling in our ears the whole way.

Our success was enough that the whole town ate hot meat that night. And through our wild excitement, I'd shared the secret smile of Hunters with my father and I knew this was what I wanted to do all my life.

Hulanna could wear beautiful dresses and walk down the aisle of flowers with a boy someday. My dresses would be the hides we scraped clean, my path the one that went through deep snow past the reaching arms of the forest ghouls.

Chapter Fourteen

It was easy to talk big around Olen. He made that easy. It was a lot harder when the sound of his lonely mandolin was in the distance and it was just me again trudging down the forest path.

I needed a plan. A blind girl with a staff, a blindfold, and a little cage wasn't much use unless she had a plan. The problem was, I thought that the Fae might be a lot smarter than I was. Any plan I made would have to account for that. So how did you trap someone who was a world-class trapper? How did you kill something who lived to kill? How did you catch the un-catchable?

If only those old wives had left tales about that. Rhymes were handy, but so far, my iron birdcage and Olen's mandolin hadn't done a whole lot of anything.

I was almost at the village when I saw the faint flutter at the edge of my sight. I'd taken the blindfold off periodically to check around me and this was the first movement I'd seen in the spirit world.

They were out there. Hunting me.

Well, that made it interesting.

I shivered. The problem was, the Fae were predators.

Beautiful predators, my mind insisted, but predators all the same.

I'd hunted predators with father before. Wolves. Coyotes. Mountain Lions. With predators, the best way to trap them was to lure them in with the cries of injured prey – now obviously we didn't hurt rabbits just to bring in wolves, but my imitation of a wounded rabbit was pretty good. Annoying, but good. And you'd tie a piece of cloth to the end of a low branch and tie a string to the branch so you could pull the string and waggle it all around and make it look like a rabbit was flopping around on the ground. I'd done that before, too.

But the Shining Ones weren't wolves or coyotes.

So, how did I lure them in? They already seemed drawn to me. They already seemed to want me and my family. So, maybe I didn't need any more bait than that.

But bait was only half my problem. The other half was actually trapping them. I had this cage. Could that do something? It was called the Cage of Souls. That seemed promising.

I kept my eyes glued to the forest, trying to look for any flicker of movement as I stood in the clearing, slowly spinning around. Was there any mention of a cage in the old stories? There was Glinda and the Magic Locket. In that story, all Glinda had to do was kiss the locket and it kept her soul safe. But that wasn't a cage. There was Jath and the Red Hood. In that Faewald story, if Jath wore the hood, he was invisible to the Faeries and could sneak through their lands. Again, not a cage.

Try as I might, I couldn't think of any cages in the old stories.

If the cage was a mystery, then I needed to rely on what I did know. I quoted the old rhyme to myself again.

Music to bind, Fire to blind, Look in their eye, With Iron they die.

Olen was doing his part at keeping them at bay with his music. I wasn't really in the condition to look anyone in the eye right now. Not with my blindfold on when I wasn't using my second sight. That left fire and iron. Only a fool would go tripping through the woods with fire in her hands. That was a great way to burn our home to the ground with a massive forest fire. But I could find iron. All my father's arrows were iron-tipped. And with the blindfold, I could still use a bow.

Determined now that I had a plan, I gave the woods around me one last look and when no one poked their head out from behind a tree, I pulled my blindfold on, took a deep breath and strode down the path toward my home. There would be arrows there. And a bow. I'd get the iron I needed and get out fast before my mother noticed me. I could just guess what she would say if she saw me – after losing my sister and now my father ...

I shivered. I'd better hurry.

I slid through the trees as quietly as I could, trying not to make a sound.

Which was how I stumbled over them without them noticing me.

I noticed Heldra first, standing stalk-still with her eyes wide and a look of ecstasy on her face. Her little sister – four-year-old Denelda – clutched her hand, but her fingers were slipping out of Heldra's grip as her other hand reached for something.

Hurriedly, I yanked the blindfold from my eyes and gasped.

There were two of the enemy.

And they were gloriously beautiful.

They looked like brothers, with the exact same mischievous, charming grins, the exact same dark hair and intricate winding tattoos up their arms and over their bare chests and rippling abdominals. Those vests did nothing to hide their forms. The wings were identical, too – like the dark wings of hawks – glorious and dangerous both at once. I recognized the way they were there and not there and then suddenly – just like last time – I blinked and all I saw were ragged torn wings with leather hanging in strips from them. Jagged belts with hunks of cloth and stinking leather formed clothing and their hair was matted, unwashed, and dirty. They stank.

Only for a moment.

And then they were back to glorious once more. One of them scooped up Denelda's flickering ghost and she clung to him, giggling, while the other took Heldra's spectral hand, drawing her to him for a passionate kiss.

They hadn't seen me, not yet. If I hurried, if I ran, maybe I could get home, grab a bow and get back in time to stop them before they brought the girls through the circle.

But that would mean putting the blindfold over my eyes and blocking out the spirit plane. Fear spiked down my spine like a falling icicle. What other choice did I have? I couldn't abandon them to the Shining Ones – not even Heldra.

With shaking hands, I pulled the blindfold over my eyes and ran.

Chapter Fifteen

Where was it? Where was it?

There! I grabbed the bow from the top shelf in the goat shed, slipping my foot between the bow and string as I pushed my weight onto the upper limb and quickly re-strung it. Good. And now arrows.

There were a few dozen shoved shaft-first into an empty barrel. I filled a leather quiver with as many as I could jam inside. They were all iron-tipped. I checked their fletchings by long habit. Good.

I spun, planning to run back out of the shed and almost ran straight into my mother. The sound she made in the back of her throat was half-howl and half-sigh, half relief and half panic.

She was blocking the door.

"Mother," I gasped. What did I say? There was too much. Best to leave it for later. "I need to get past you."

"Allie Hunter!" She shook with emotion. "Alastra Hunter, don't you dare take a step! Don't you dare! Where were you all night? I was so worried. Your father ..."

She swallowed a moan, her hand covering her mouth and her face crumpling in pain. Awkwardly, I reached for her as she shook with contained sobs. It took her a moment to finish shaking in my awkward half-hug before she pulled away, her face schooling itself to calm.

"He went after you! He went into the circle!"

"I know," I said.

"You *know?*" The betrayal in her voice cut me to the quick.

"I saw Olen. He told me. But I can't stay and talk. I have to go. The Fae have Heldra and Denelda. And if I don't catch up to them, they'll take them, too!"

"You knew and you didn't come straight home," she sounded gutted.

"I just found out," I said, trying to be calm. Trying not to let her re-spark that fear. If it started again, I wasn't sure I could burn it away this time. "And I have to go after the Thatcher girls. I'm Hunter now, Mother."

"I thought you were blind, Alastra!" She didn't sound angry anymore. She sounded terrified. "How do you plan to hunt them without your sight? You can't just leave me again when you've only just returned!"

"I'll explain later, Mother. I don't have time now!" No time for all these emotions, either. "But your grandmother's scarf – it works! It helps me see!"

I pushed past her – a girl on a mission. Her hand closed around my arm, pulling me back.

"Where did you find that cage? That's not ... it's not the Cage of Souls, is it?"

"Maybe," I said a little guiltily. There was something about her tone – like she thought I was doing something wrong.

She closed her eyes and took a deep breath. Maybe she was burning away emotions, too. Because when she was done, she opened her eyes and peace ruled her features again.

"There's a price to that," she said. "A price to use it."

"Then I'll just have to pay the price, won't I?" I said. But I was just a bit worried. What kind of price did you pay? No time for that. I burned that worry away, feeding it into the fire of my determination. I'd pay the price I had to pay.

"Let me," she said a little breathlessly. "Let me do it for you."

I sighed. "You're not much of a hunter, Mother, you know that. You can't even track the goats. You could shoot all day and never hit the target. I'm Hunter now that father is gone. This is my job. And I'll be good at it."

She was clearly torn, still wanting to take the cage from me, but swayed by my words. I leaned in close and hugged her fiercely, wishing I could stay with her, wishing I could let her do this for me, protect me, shelter me. But I couldn't. This was my task. My trial. My redemption.

"Please, Allie. Please, take care." A tiny dent had formed in her forehead.

"I promise," I whispered, hugging her one last time, before slipping out into the night. And I wasn't sure if I was lying or not.

Chapter Sixteen

I crept through the woods, trying to be fast and careful at the same time. Every time I slipped the blindfold off, I could see their trail – smoky and dark in seductive swirls and tangles through the trees. At one point, a second tangled black trail joined them. It wasn't black so much as it was the opposite of light – like a living dark.

I had to put the blindfold back on frequently to navigate the trails without stumbling. The back and forth was giving me a headache and it was nearly sunset in the forest. The Fae had not headed straight for the circle of Star Stones as I'd expected. They'd headed toward the mountains I'd started from at dawn.

My legs ached from all the walking and my throat burned. I needed a drink of water and something to eat. But Hunters didn't whine about missing meals or burning throats. They were one with the land. They were the hands of the land as they managed the herds and limited predators. And that was what I was doing tonight – limiting predators.

What were they doing up this mountain? What were they thinking? I needed to get into their minds. If only it was as easy for me as it seemed to be for them to get into mine!

If they weren't taking the girls to the Star Stones to exchange them for the freedom of more Shining Ones, then why had they taken them?

That 'why' rang uncomfortably in my head over and over again.

What did the stories say about the Shining Ones wanted?

There was the story of nine-toed Noris who had been enchanted by Faeries to dance until all his toes fell off, but after losing just one of them, he fell into a well and died dancing at the bottom. There was the story of Ella the Enchanted who had been enchanted by Faeries to think that stones were frosted cakes until she ate so many that she fell down and died. There was the story of the Empty Houses in which Faeries had visited a village and stolen the children out of their beds from every home that had failed to leave out a saucer of milk for them.

But did any of those lead me closer to the truth?

They told me one thing very plainly. The Shining Ones had a great sense of humor, if killing people in cruel ways seemed funny to you. And they loved sweets and dancing and fun – if you looked past the fact that they also loved killing people with them. And they loved to instill terror in people. They fed off it. It made them laugh.

I shivered.

What terror were they going to inflict on the Thatcher girls? What terror were they inflicting on my father? My sister?

I chewed my lip as I worked my way up the mountain.

There was a glow from a fire up above me on a narrow ledge on the side of the mountain. The silhouette of someone dancing made dark shadows flicker and careen across the surrounding rocks. I crept forward slowly, taking an arrow from my quiver and nocking it on the string. I didn't pull back yet. No point weakening the string – or my arms – before I was ready.

I slipped my belt through the handle of the Cage of Souls and tightened it around my waist and then carefully pulled the blindfold down around my neck.

Okay. I was ready.

Just in time.

When the screaming began, I scrambled upward, feeling with my hands so that I wouldn't hit a rock or tree. I didn't dare pull the blindfold up again. Didn't dare miss what might be my only shot. I had to get to them before they danced off the ledge or ate stones – or whatever other awful thing the Shining Ones had in store. I gritted my teeth together and scrambled harder over the loose shale as the screams became more high-pitched and desperate.

Denelda was only a child. Only a child! They'd better not be hurting her, or they'd bristle so badly with arrows that people would be calling them 'Mr. Porcupine' for the rest of their lives – which would be short.

I saw the little girl first, her hands tied over her head, suspending her in the air over the roaring fire. Her sister – Heldra – danced wildly in front of the fire, her feet already tired, but when she slowed, the rope lowered and if she sped up, it pulled the little girl up again. How long could Heldra keep this up? Already her feet stumbled as she danced. Her breathing was ragged, and her eyes glazed over with concentration. It hadn't taken long to wear her down. It wouldn't take much longer to break her.

Okay, the predators were occupied with their squealing rabbit. I counted three. The two with the hawk wings that I'd seen before and one other with smoky black wings. Now was my chance.

With care, I raised my bow, but I couldn't see the bow with the blindfold on. Frustrated, I pulled the blindfold off. But with it gone, the Fae disappeared. They must work some charm so that the humans they interacted with could see them when they wanted to be seen but not when they didn't. And right now, they only wanted Heldra and Denelda looking at them.

But if I fired off an arrow without seeing them, I'd be sure to miss. And if I couldn't see the bow and the arrow at all, I could hit Heldra or Denelda. *Tsking* under my breath, I pulled the blindfold over one eye but not the other.

Okay. I looked ridiculous, and it might slip at any time – and it was giving me the worst headache I'd ever had – but this was my only shot. I nocked the arrow again and carefully brought it up, ready to draw back.

One of the Fae was missing. There were only two where there had been three only a moment ago. My heart sped up. One holding Denelda's rope. One taunting Heldra. It was the one with the black smoke wings – the one who had tried to seduce me in the forest. He was the one who was missing.

I scanned the stone landscape around them and looked up and down the path, but there was nothing to see there.

Cursing quietly, I drew the bowstring back. There were still two to deal with. This was my chance to dispatch them. I focused on the one taunting Heldra, trying to see true through dizzy eyes which could not agree on what they were seeing, steadying my breath, being sure of my target and what was beyond it, making sure I didn't pull when I released.

I took the shot.

The Shining One dropped to the ground.

And then everything happened at once.

Heldra screamed. Denelda began to fall, her little voice shrieking in terror. The Fae holding her rope leapt forward.

I pulled another arrow from my quiver, nocking it carefully, drawing quickly, begging my hands to stop shaking, and taking a deep breath.

I released.

Something gripped my shoulder with an icy hand just as I released. My arrow went wide, the blood freezing in my veins.

I spun and there he was, a wicked smile on his face. He bit his lower lip in a tempting fashion as if it was just him and I in those woods and he wanted to be an entirely different kind of predator. The drumming of my heart was faster than a partridge's wings. Out of control. Not just from fear, now, but from fascination and excitement, too. The blindfold slipped off my face the rest of the way and he swam into perfect clarity.

"Little Mortal," he purred. "I remember you. The Lady wants you, Little Hunter. She was ... specific."

The way he said 'specific' sent little chills up and down my spine.

"Don't stay with these blind people, Little Hunter. Come to me."

He beckoned with his long finger, licking his delicious upper lip as he watched me. Did he think I was edible? Or did that tempt other people?

It should be tempting me. I had a feeling he was using all his glamor on me.

He flexed subtly so that glistening muscles leapt to the surface of his skin, rippling all down his midsection where it showed through his open close-fitting jacket. He'd left that unbuttoned as if to emphasize his lithe form. I felt a little flutter in my belly.

He was beautiful. He made me look like an old raggedy doll beside him. Something abandoned by feckless children. He made me dull and thick beside his brilliance. Sad and miserable against his hedonistic delight. He wouldn't have missed that shot. He wouldn't need a staff to walk through the woods. He was perfect.

But something was nagging at me.

He was distracting me. He was trying to keep my gaze away from something. First, the lip-biting, then the licking, now the flexing. What was he trying to hide?

My eyes narrowed.

Music to bind, Fire to blind, Look in their eye, With Iron they die.

My gaze shot up, catching his unaware so that he flinched, his eyes going wide.

I held his gaze.

Moments flicked past like leaves whipping from a tree in a strong wind and as they passed, that gaze we shared began to bare him before my new sight. First, the glamor fell. The brocade trousers, leather boots, and silver belt buckle fell away to nothing but rags and bones and rawhide cords. He was nothing but a skinny, fox-faced creature with matted hair and a hungry look that seemed to be eating him up from the inside. And something more – something darker rippled beneath the surface, as if even now he was still hiding a worse, darker nature.

I kept his gaze locked with mine as his eyes took on a red gleam. The look that had seemed sinfully delicious before suddenly just felt hungry, wanting, desperate. I fumbled for the cage, pulling it from my belt and lifting it up like a lantern.

He shied away from it, but our gazes stayed locked. It was as if he couldn't look away first, as if just by seeing him I was stealing his power.

And I was, wasn't I? Because they lived off notoriety. They oozed charm to make us think they were above us.

They lived off wanting. They made us believe they could grant all our wishes and weave us into dreams.

They lived off fear. They drank it in like wine.

The more powerful the emotion, the more they were alive with it.

But looking at him like this, as he now began to ripple and tatter like his black smoke wings, as the core of his soul began to show – black and inky – through his slowly translucing skin, I wasn't afraid. And I didn't want him or what he promised. And I didn't believe the rumors that he was better than me, more beautiful, more worthy.

The glamor was gone.

As his wings shriveled and his flesh faded, I could see his tiny blackened soul.

"You're nothing but smoke," I breathed. "Nothing but the ashes of something once alive."

And it must have been those words that did it, because nothing else changed. I said the words and then he winked out of existence like a dream ending.

"Well," I said, "that was anticlimactic."

"You think so?" a velvet voice asked, and it was all I could do not to yelp.

Where was the voice coming from?

"I find it rather magical. Wickedly magical. Can I tempt you to set me free? There are things I could do for you ... things that would make every second of my freedom worth your while."

The voice was coming from the cage and as I lowered it, I saw that the door had shut itself and inside – trying very hard not to touch the bars around the outside – the Fae stood. He was a small version of himself – small enough to fit in the cage but as beautiful as he had been with all his glamor working its way with me.

I'd trapped him!

My eyes grew wide at the sight.

I had him in the Cage of Souls!

Now what?

A child's scream pierced the air and quick as I could, I pulled my blindfold back up and snatched up my bow and jammed it in the quiver. This wasn't over. There were still more of them out there.

Chapter Seventeen

I scrambled up the hill, ignoring the commentary from the little cage I'd strapped back on my belt.

"Could you stop jostling me? I don't like touching iron!"

Like I was worried about his comfort with a child screaming nearby!

"You know we can read thoughts if they're on the top of your mind, right? I can hear you not caring about me!"

I stuck out a mental tongue and hurried forward, using my staff to feel the path ahead of me as I tried to watch where I was going with one eye and search for the escaped Fae with the other eye.

I found Heldra and Denelda first. Heldra held her sister tight to her chest, tears pouring down her face as she drew in long ragged breaths.

"Heldra!" I gasped. "Is she okay?"

"I should have known you'd be involved in this!" Heldra accused me. "You and your sister are both Faerie-sent!"

I clenched my jaw. Could she just keep her thoughts to herself so we could help her sister? The way she said it though – it reminded me of a voice I'd heard. The voice of someone talking to Olen in the forest. About me.

Fuel, Allie! Use it to fuel you.

"Denelda," I said through clenched teeth. "Is she hurt?"

The little girl was wailing, but whether from fear or from harm I couldn't tell. She pointed a small finger toward my feet.

"It moved!" she wailed.

I looked down as the Fae – glassy-eyed but still breathing – twitched again. It was the first one I'd shot, and I'd hit him in the torso, but I hadn't hit him well enough to kill him. I must have struck spine. Though his hands jerked and twitched, his lower half was still. I swallowed down bile.

He'd lost his glamor when he was hit, and he stank of old goats and rotting meat.

"Your fault, Little Hunter!" The Fae in the cage hissed at me. "Nuuli didn't deserve a death like this. You're angry that we scared a child? That's adorable. You killed someone! Killer! Murderer!"

"I thought you were immortal," I muttered.

"What?" Heldra asked loudly.

"I'm just talking to the fool in the cage," I said, flicking it with my finger, but my eyes stayed on the Fae twitching on the ground. Did he look ... stronger? The arrow popped out of his chest.

"What fool? That cage is empty. You're crazy Allie Hunter! Crazier than ever. You made all this happen!"

His eyes were less glassy.

He blinked and looked at me, smiling in a way that curved his perfect lips into a perfect bow. Wait. Hadn't he lost his glamor?

"Murderer! Murderer!" the Fae in the cage whispered.

But I wasn't going to let him distract me any more than Heldra's curses and threats. That Fae was coming back to life.

How had I done this last time? I pulled the blindfold all the way down and as Heldra and her sister faded to ghosts, the

Fae jumped into full color and I locked my gaze with his, really seeing.

"You're nothing but an old story," I told him. "And I've had enough of stories."

And just like that, I had two Fae in my cage.

I pulled the blindfold up in time to see a sobbing Heldra running down the mountain path, her sister still clutched to her chest.

In the darkness, a shadow seemed to flicker on her path.

I yanked my blindfold down just in time to see one of his feathered wings as he darted out of sight.

This wasn't over.

Chapter Eighteen

Heldra was as lost as I had been before I discovered the blindfold. She stumbled and wove through the trees, her ragged breathing so loud that I could have followed it from a mile away.

But in the darkness, I was having problems of my own. My head pounded from switching back and forth from first and second sight too much. I was dizzy and unsteady in my steps and the faster I went, the faster Heldra went, as if she was fleeing me as well as the Fae stalking her.

My throat was raw from thirst, and the voices in my little cage were driving me crazy.

"If I were you, I'd just give in. Life with us will be more exciting for your friend."

"Is that what you call fearing for your life?" I muttered. "Exciting?"

"Beats being trapped in a cage."

"What do you want to bet?"

"My life?"

He was hilarious. Just a cage full of laughs.

The Fae chasing Heldra was playing with her, like a cat with a mouse. Leaping out one way and then popping out of a shadow in the other direction. If someone had excellent hearing and a bat's ability to pinpoint a sound's exact location, they could have followed Heldra's little shrieks and made a map of the path – or lack of path – between the mountain and the circle of Star Stones.

We had grown slowly closer and closer as the night closed in, until there was no light left but the silver of the moon when the clouds parted.

The smell of the pines retreating and the balmy heather of the mountain plains advancing should have been comforting. How many times had I smelled that very smell when following my father in the hunt? But it was anything but calming tonight.

The sound of the faint mandolin in the distance was worse. We were getting close. And if this last Fae managed to get Heldra and her sister into the circle, how many Fae would come pouring through that gap. One for one, was the legend. But legends weren't always true, were they? I'd been getting a crash course in that.

After all, if two sisters go out walking in the woods and one is taken by evil, the other one always manages to save her. And I hadn't saved my sister.

If a maid fair and innocent is stolen by evil magic, a handsome prince always wakes her up. But where was the prince on the grand charger riding in to save Hulanna? My father had gone. And he hadn't come back again.

I clenched my jaw and stumbled on, almost colliding with a dark shadow.

"Oh," Olen said, relief filling his voice. "It's just you. I thought I heard crying."

"The mandolin," I said through stunned lips. When had the music stopped? I'd thought I'd heard it just a moment ago.

He spoke with a smile. "I don't need to play music all the time, do I?"

He was beautiful. More beautiful than I remembered. Even with one eye covered with the blindfold, all I saw was his better, spirit-self instead of the usual blotchy ... wait ... wait. No. Both my eyes were covered. So why was I seeing ... was that mandolin I heard playing? And an awkward voice singing an ancient folk tune?

"O come to me by midnight, my love, my love! O come to me..."

Glamor!

I gasped and then the not-Olen stepped forward quickly and slapped a hand over my mouth. He was strong – strong enough to grab one of my arms and pin it to my back, pushing it too high so that I had to stand on my tiptoes, tears pricking my eyes.

"I thought to myself, why bring two when you can have three," he whispered in my ear and his cheek brushing mine pulled the blindfold down and with it, my sight evaporated.

He shoved me forward and I stumbled blindly through the rocks and heather, arm pinned behind my back.

The Star Stone circle glowed bright ahead of me. The rocks forming it seemed to be speckled with stars as if they were pieces of the night sky. And inside the ring, the hungry prisoners reached toward us with craving hands.

Heldra and Denelda flickered in and out of my vision – barely-there ghosts in this world that wasn't meant for the living. And there was no sign of Olen near the circle. I frowned, confused. I could almost swear that I still heard mandolin in the distance, but why would Olen leave the circle when he'd sworn to protect it? That wasn't like him – not dedicated, certain Olen.

I swallowed.

"Now, let the others go," the Fae whispered in my ear.

"Your friends?" I asked. "I'm afraid they're stuck in the little cage forever."

I didn't know that. But he didn't either.

"Oh, I don't mean them," he laughed nastily in my ear. "Oh no, didn't they tell you? Fae don't have friends. We have ... competitors."

"Then who do you want me to let go?" I spat.

"The girls. Let them go through the stones. Don't try to stop them. The Lady wants them. And what the Lady wants, she gets."

"I don't know your Lady," I said, sweat pouring down my forehead from the pain in my arm. Heldra's flickering ghost was getting closer and closer to the ring. They'd eat her and her sister alive.

"Oh, but I think you do. I think you know her very well indeed."

The crowd in the circle was in uproar. A mass of horns and wings and tails and gnashing teeth and fluttering wings – like if you tried to trap every creature in the world in a single net. It pushed against the imaginary boundary and then some along the edges were pulled down into the earth as if into a great pit. Those from the middle shoved outward and I had a sense that someone important had arrived and space was being made for them.

The Lady, perhaps?

There was a flicker of light and then all of a sudden loud folk music was pouring over me as Olen – bright and beautiful

– charged toward us. He grabbed the flickering ghosts of Heldra and Denelda, spinning them toward the forest.

"That way," he ordered, panic in his voice. "That way!"

But in his panic, he'd stopped singing.

The Shining One behind me whispered, "Freeze."

And just like that, the three of them froze. Olen's spirit eyes watched us with wide, frozen horror.

"And just like that, there's four. But they don't have to be whole to go through the circle. They just have to be alive."

"Don't hurt them," I begged. Olen's wide eyes were mirrored by the ghostly flickering eyes of Denelda. "Don't hurt them and I'll talk to your Lady."

"Afraid?" he asked me, delight dancing in his tone.

And I knew I shouldn't be afraid – didn't dare be afraid. I was supposed to take that fear and let it fuel me, not let it fill me like cold water seeping into drowning lungs.

But I was.

"You should be afraid," he said with a delighted smile. "When I'm done with them, you won't know which is which. But first, let's make sure you don't go anywhere, yes?"

And with a snap like a dried twig, he broke the arm that he was gripping.

Pain flooded over me and I bit my lip hard, tasting blood and hardly caring, as I sank to my knees. He was inhumanly fast. One breath and he was in front of Olen's frozen form, pulverizing him with punches that looked like iron hitting leather.

Iron.

Music to bind, Fire to blind, Look in their eye, With Iron they die.

With a wail, I pulled myself to my feet, ignoring the blinding pain in my arm and the fact that all I could see were Fae, and Olen, and the flickering forms of the girls. With my good arm, I reached into my quiver, drew an arrow out and leapt forward, plunging it into the back of the Shining One. It was hardly even a stab. More like a prod.

But it didn't require brute strength. It required iron. Iron in the arrow and iron in the mind.

"You're a fraud," I gasped between stabs of pain. "You wear the face of another. And you aren't taking anyone into that circle with you tonight."

The Cage of Souls flashed and then there were three in its depths.

I sighed with relief as Heldra and her sister moved, no longer frozen by Fae magic.

"Run, Heldra!" I gasped.

Olen slumped painfully to the ground, at an angle so uncomfortable that he had to be badly injured.

"Olen?" I was just leaning over him, checking to be sure he was alive, when a crystal voice rang out.

"Allie? Can you hear me?"

My heart stuttered in my chest.

Chapter Nineteen

When I was four years old, Hulanna gave me her teddy bear because mine fell in the fire. Even though it was her favorite. Even though my parents couldn't afford to replace it.

She had loved me that much.

Chapter Twenty

My head whipped up.

Hulanna?

In my little Cage of Souls, my captives laughed as my heart lurched.

"Allie," her voice was different. It was commanding and tinkling at the same time. Thrilling and terrifying.

Was that really her?

I stood up straight, cradling my broken arm with my other hand.

She stood straight, too, but with an army of Fae at her back. How was she here and not imprisoned by them? Had father found her? Were they both coming back? Hope surged through me and I took an unconscious step forward.

And then I saw the crown. It was pale silver but glittering with diamonds. Woven in thin tendrils like dew-encrusted grass, it almost swayed in the breeze. A thing of magic and artistry. A thing of betrayal.

I gasped.

"Time works differently here," Hulanna said, but the smile she gave me was not the smile I was used to. It was icy cold and proud. Her red hair – so much like mine, was dark auburn now. "For you, it has only been days. For me, years have passed."

My twin. In so many ways like me. And yet, not like me at all.

"Where is Father?" I asked, cringing at how small my voice sounded in my own ears.

Less than her, it seemed to say. Less than all of them. Worthless. Small. Useless. Hopeless.

"Forget about him."

"I won't." But my defiance sounded weak in my ears. I couldn't find anything to fuel it. Not even fear.

"Come with us, Allie. Come with us and leave this pitiful place. You were never meant for *here*."

The sneer in her voice stung, but not as much as the betrayal. Not as much as the casual way she dismissed our father's life when he had gone after her without a second thought.

I looked in her eyes.

"You're small," I said.

And then she flickered. And she was my Hulanna again for a fraction of a second, looking cold and scared and alone with a ring of dirty feathers around her head instead of a crown, her mouth hanging open uncertainly.

I gasped.

"Come home," I choked out, my voice cracking at the sight of her shivering in the mud with all those cruel faces behind her. My fear shifted at the sight of her – the fire beginning to stir.

And then the glamor slammed back into place and she was once again cold and regal.

"Never," she said. "But you will come to me."

"No." And my words were iron. The iron of a Hunter on her homeland. The fire licked at my fear, burning it away.

"Not now, perhaps. But soon."

"No." Harder iron. The Iron of being one with the bones of the land.

"Sooner than you realize."

And then they all winked out of the circle, and the light of the world went with them.

I ran forward. I didn't know what I was thinking. I was a fool to run into the very circle that had eaten my sister and my father, but run I did, stumbling over stones and dips in the ground until I finally fell completely, breaking my fall with my good hand and getting a mouthful of bracken for my trouble. I pulled myself to my feet.

The Cage of Souls clattered against the rocks as I scrambled up. My arm was fire and agony, but I ignored it, desperate to see what had happened. Had it worked?

I was standing inside the ring of Star Stone. Standing there just as if there had never been a door here to another world. I'd half-hoped I wouldn't go through. Half-hoped I wouldn't plunge into Faewald. I'd betrayed myself with that half-hope.

Because now there was no way to the other side, and that meant that for my father and sister, there was no way back.

"Lost your chance," a little voice said from the cage. "Does that make you feel small?"

Tears filled my eyes, splashing hot down my cheeks. I bit my lip, drifting on the cold pain of my arm and the hot stabs of my guilt until an arm wrapped over my shoulder. Sort of wrapped – sort of leaned. Olen coughed beside me. The weak, shallow cough of someone who was hurting too much to cough deeply.

I looked up into his perfect spirit face.

"I lost," I said. Even my voice sounded lost.

"I don't know about that," he pursed his lips. "Sometimes when you seem like you've lost, it's only because you're beginning to win. What's with the cage hanging from your belt. Were you out birding?"

He hadn't seen them – I realized. Not Hulanna. Not the Fae in the circle. He'd only seen the one who hit him – the one that was now in my cage.

I glanced down at the Cage of Souls and at the three brooding occupants. I had, indeed, lost. But maybe I still had the keys I needed to win tomorrow. If I dared to use them.

"Either way," Olen said, coughing hollowly. "I need your help tracking down a healer, Hunter. The Thatcher girls are long gone and I don't trust my own feet to get me to safety. Think that you're up for the job?"

His tone was light, but the way he stood suggested that he was hurting as badly as I was. And the way he kept looking longingly at the stones told me he was as torn as I was.

"I can hunt anything down," I said, glancing over my shoulder as we slowly helped each other out of the circle again. "And when this arm heals, I'm going to prove it."

I looked back at the circle as we entered the forest and that look was a promise. Somewhere in there my sister and father were waiting, and Allie Hunter was going to go get them.

This still wasn't over.

BOOK TWO

Music to bind,
Fire to blind,
Look in their eye,
With Iron they die.
-Tales of the Faewald

In a ring but deep you go,
In a spot the wind can't blow,
Buried deep but not in dirt,
Hold your breath, with death you flirt.
-Tales of the Faewald

Chapter Twenty-One

When I was a child of ten, Hulanna and I kept rabbits. We fed them the bright sunny dandelions that grew in the field and handfuls of thick grass.

One day I went to feed my rabbit, but it was gone.

"Hulanna!" I'd called in a panic. "They're gone! Someone stole our rabbits!"

"They weren't stolen," Hulanna said. "I gave them to the Travelers. They stopped by here today to see Mother."

"Why!" I could feel my eyes stinging with tears. "Why would you do that?"

"One of them read my future and she showed it to me in a magic ball," Hulanna said with a dreamy smile. "She said I would marry a lord so beautiful that it stung my eyes, with a land far away from here so powerful that it bound me to it forever, and riches so plentiful that I would never want to leave."

"And you gave them my rabbit?"

She looked me firmly in the eye her lips trembling. "I gave them mine. But they told me it was one girl for each rabbit. And if I wanted you to have the same fate, I'd have to give them your rabbit. I didn't want to go far away without you, Allie. I wanted you to share my fate. So I gave them your rabbit and they gave you my fate."

I was angry about the rabbit. But if I had been a little bit wiser, I would have known that what I should have been furious about was the fate. For she bound me to it, though I didn't realize it then, and I was sold as surely as the rabbits.

Chapter Twenty-Two

I woke to a pounding headache and darkness. I felt hot and feverish, my mind seeming to twist as I clawed for coherent thought. Frantic, I sat up, biting back a shriek at the blinding pain that shot through my arm.

Oh yes. I'd broken my arm. The events around the Star Stone circle came crashing back into my mind and I flinched at the memory of my sister – the Lady of the Faewald.

I looked around with bleary eyes, but without the blindfold, I could see nothing but darkness and faint trails through the room – and my Cage of Souls sitting on the table at the center of the kitchen. Moaning in pain from my arm, I walked gingerly to the table, hoping I wouldn't stub a toe on the furniture.

I could hear voices outside, but they weren't clear enough to make out. Murmurs and growls. Or maybe that was my imagination again. My head hurt so much that it easily could be.

The Fae I had captured were still in the cage. I leaned in close so that I could see them through my bleary eyes. They were just as they had been in the outside world, but miniature – no larger than the length of my hand, huddled away from the bars.

"Little Hunter," one of them acknowledged as I approached. He stood with arms crossed over his chest and a look of disgust on his face. "You put us in an iron cage."

His glamor was flickering in and out. One moment he was a gorgeous specimen of masculinity, the next the strange bone-and-rags feral creature underneath.

"You're still here," I breathed.

"Where did you think we would go?" he lifted an eyebrow, gesturing to the cage bars. His movements were startlingly fluid and just a little too fast. Had I noticed that before?

His companions didn't look quite as well. One of them lay on the ground, twitching like a dying bird. The other had pulled my arrow from his thigh, but he hunched over his fellow and growled at me like a beast.

"I had planned to set you free into the Star Stone circle," I said. A look of hope sprang up on the crouched Fair Folk's face. "But it's closed now. I can't get you in."

I could still remember walking away last night. It had been cold and dark, and I'd had to help Olen walk. Even with my arm broken, I was in better shape than he was. We'd caught up to Heldra and Denelda quickly and Heldra cursed me every time he let out a moan, but she couldn't help him with a traumatized Denelda in her arms. I hadn't been able to do much with a broken arm. I'd had to tie the bow and cage to my back. My arm was useless to me.

We'd arrived at my house first and my mother – frantic – had run for Goodie Herben. By the time she was back, she had Thatcher, Goodie Thatcher, Goodie Chanter and Baker with her.

"What have you done, you changeling child?" Goodie Thatcher had asked me. I didn't even bother answering. She'd already made up her mind about me and my arm burned with pain.

Goodie Herben had patched up Heldra and Denelda – they'd mostly been bruised and shaken – and then Goodie Thatcher had taken them home, breathing threats to me until she was out the door.

"You'll not be Hunter for our village as long as I have breath! This was all your scheme for the role. You've killed your father and older sister just to get it. You don't fool me. I'll see justice served and my girls repaid!"

We'd all been too worried about Olen to listen. It had taken Thatcher and Baker to carry him home and Goodie Herben had gone with them. Her face was pale as she left. I'd rarely seen it pale – not since the time she'd midwifed at the farm next door and come to us for goat's milk. My mother had asked about Goodie Weaver who was birthing that night and Goodie Herben had shaken her head and when mother asked about the infant, she'd looked that same way as when she was tending Olen. We'd helped Weaver bury his wife and new daughter the next day and mother had sent Hulanna to his house with hot meals every night for a solid month.

I swallowed at the memory.

A tiny snapping sound brought my attention back to the Fae in the cage. The angry standing Fae was snapping his fingers at me.

"While our suffering seems not to concern you, mortal hunter, I would think you could at least offer water. We are, after all, dying."

"Dying?" I asked, shocked.

He gave me a pitying look like you might give a particularly stupid child and pointed at the Fae twitching on the floor of the cage.

"What would you call that?"

"I thought you were immortal," I countered.

"It's like you don't even know the rules of the Faewald," he hissed.

I snorted, feeling around now for my blindfold. There it was. Around my neck. I pulled it up and went in search of my mother's sewing kit. There was a thimble in there that could hold water for the Fae.

Our cottage was oddly unkempt. My mother usually kept it clean and neat so that not a thing was out of place, but her bedclothes were rumpled, a wooden cup askew on the table, the water barrel was half empty and her nightclothes were scattered on the bed. Odd.

I passed a hand over my forehead. I was burning with fever. Not good.

Maybe Mother was checking on Olen. Maybe he was worse.

I found the sewing kit and filled the thimble and a wooden cup with water from the barrel and pulled my blindfold off to offer it to the Fae.

"Here," I said, holding it out to the Leader. I couldn't help it – it was how I thought of him. After all, he was the one doing all the talking.

"Could you pass it through the bars?" he asked tightly.

I rolled my eyes. "Just because you are used to having humans dance to your will doesn't mean I plan to serve you."

"The iron burns us," he hissed. "And this cage surrounds us in iron."

"I'd feel so bad for you," I said, setting the thimble down outside the cage – where he could reach it if he really wanted to. "If you hadn't stolen my father and sister and hurt my best friend."

"They came to us willingly," he said, his glamor flickering.

"Just like you'll pick up that cup willingly," I countered, taking a drink from my own cup and splashing my face with the cold water.

I put my blindfold back on and the Fae winked out. Though a few minutes later, I saw the thimble inside the cage instead of outside.

The sounds outside the cottage were getting louder and combined with my missing mother were making me worried.

I dressed with a great deal of pain and trouble. I chose hunting leathers this time and high leather boots that went midway up my thigh. I couldn't rebraid my hair, so I left that a mess. Grabbing the bow would be a waste of time. I couldn't draw it like this. Couldn't do anything useful at all.

I blew a strand of hair out of my face, huffed at it and opened the door of my cottage.

Chapter Twenty-Three

When we were seven, my mother made us a treat for Springtide night.

I had been looking forward to Springtide for months. It was the singing that I loved best and while Hulanna – whose voice was as lovely as a calling bird – was dreaming of sweets and of showing off her dark red curls in the new way she was styling them, I was dreaming of the hour the whole town would stand around the central well and sing by candlelight. It was like a choir of angels. One angelic moment in the year.

We would sing the song that kept the ghouls away from the town – restricting them to the forest. This year, we'd already lost two goats to the ghouls. They had sucked out their blood in the night while we were sleeping. Goats couldn't defend themselves – not from blood-sucking shadows. And our goats weren't the only ones. We needed the Springtide songs to hold the predators back.

I was practicing my singing while I washed the dishes when my mother came out with a blanket in her hands and a huge smile on her face and my father put down the bow string he was oiling with a matching smile as he joined her.

"We have a surprise," my mother said, practically glowing.

"What is it?" Hulanna asked. She had been daydreaming instead of drying the dishes and her towel was barely even damp as the stack of clean dishes grew beside her.

My mother opened the apron and pulled out two white lace-edged aprons to our delight. Hulanna squealed, rushing to hug her as my father and I shared a shy smile.

"For tonight," was what my mother said.

Hulanna put hers on right away. And she looked lovely as a snow-capped mountain, her face glowing as brightly as my mother's.

Which made it even more devastating when, an hour later, she stood too close to the fire and scorched her apron, leaving a long brown streak across the front. She turned her liquid eyes to me, tears filling them and showed me the apron.

"It's alright," I said, bravely. "We can switch. You can wear mine tonight."

And though she protested, her protests were weak. She wanted to look perfect.

I kept my face brave and merry when we went to Springtide that night. My parent's pride helped ease the pain of the scorched apron, but I still kept it hidden under my cloak.

The only time my face fell was when Goodie Alebren said in a loud voice to Hulanna, "You're certainly the prettiest girl we've ever seen in these parts – and that heavenly voice! So lovely! Such a shame your twin isn't identical to you!"

I was never what they wanted, because what they wanted was Hulanna. And I was only Allie.

Chapter Twenty-Four

My mouth dropped open when I opened the door of the cottage. It looked like the entire town was there and to my shock, Goodie Thatcher had my mother by the collar and was practically shaking as she ranted in my mother's face.

"You'll pay, Genda! You'll pay for this! My Heldra, my sweet girl, she's completely shaken and it's your family's fault!"

There were murmurs of agreement in the crowd.

"We'll send Quickstep to the Lowlands to fetch the Knights of Light!" someone suggested. Because of course, the Knights loved to go to backwoods villages and put Goodwives in their places. That's what they lived for.

I looked out, trying to see who was here, but it was harder to see who wasn't. I swallowed down fear as I saw almost every face I knew in the flickering of the torches. It wasn't morning yet, though by the faint line of light on the horizon, it would be soon.

They couldn't even wait a full night before they come to my mother's house with torches and an angry mob? Petty, small-minded people.

As if my mother hadn't already lost enough. As if any of this was her fault. I felt anger brimming up in me and I tried to shove it down. Abruptly a raven screamed, launching up from the trees and into the night sky. I took that moment to speak.

"Haven't we already paid?" I asked loudly. "Isn't losing Hulanna and Hunter enough?"

"Not even close," Goodie Thatcher said, but she'd dropped mother's collar as she spun to turn her sights on me instead.

My mother's eyes shot a warning to me as she straightened her rumpled collar. The rest of her was neat as a pin despite the shock of having the village turn up at her door. The shock had been in the cottage where she'd left things out of place.

"Because of you and your *bad seed* of a sister, our village has no Hunter. And no Chanter! Olen is broken and battered and Goodie Herben says it will be long weeks before he can Chant for us again. Do you realize what this means?"

"Ghouls," I agreed. But only because I didn't want to say "Fae" out loud.

Around her, the crowd murmured – a worried sound of people whose hard-working lives had just seen an unforeseen setback. The sound of people anxious that more work might be coming – or worse, more difficulty. It was as familiar a feeling to me as the scent of the pine trees around us as they danced in the wind or the paleness of the moonlight that sent long shadows across the goat pen. It was the feeling of Skundton in trouble. The icy feeling we'd shared when the Mattervine had flooded two springs ago and washed away grazing land. The raw feeling when the winter five years ago was too harsh for the usual traders to brave the storms with needed goods from the lowlands.

I swallowed.

"It means that the deaths of our children will be on your head," Goodie Thatcher said. "When we starve from lack of meat and invaders come to kill us all because there is no Hunter here, that will have been your fault!"

"Forget the Hunter!" Someone called. "We're sending for the Knights!"

"There is a Hunter here," I said calmly. What I wanted was to take fat Goodie Thatcher with her fine aprons and condescending looks and use her to thatch my shed. What I wanted was to scream at all these people that I had my own problems. That they should do their share to help instead of coming here and blaming my mother and me. But I pushed it all down. Fuel. I needed to let it fuel me.

Olen was hurt. And they were right. Without at least one of us, they had no defense from the Faewald or from the three Fae I had hidden inside my cottage. They didn't even have defenses from the ghouls or bears or other everyday threats. They needed me.

"Our Hunter went into the Star Stone circle!" Goodie Thatcher insisted. "There won't be roasted coneys for anyone this week. Our animals will go undefended. Our pastures made vulnerable!"

"I am Hunter for this town," I said grimly. "And I will bring in coneys and deal with predators."

"You? The blind girl?" Goodie Thatcher's laugh was harsh, and behind her, I saw Heldra snickering with her mother. Really, Heldra? I could have left her to dance her feet off. I could have walked away, but no, I had to go and save the life of that ungrateful goat.

"What can *you* do?" Heldra sneered.

"Watch and see," I said.

I turned and opened the door of the cottage and strode back inside. I'd have to set snares today, despite my arm. I could do that one-handed though the work would be slow.

I strode to the chest in the back that had my father's hunting things, dragged out his snares and began to stuff them in a gunny sack. There was wire there, and with care, I sat at the table and began to mend any weak points and examine the snares. I'd begin as soon as I had them laid out.

After long minutes my mother came into the house and shut the door with a relieved sigh. The sounds of the crowd outside didn't follow her inside. They must have dispersed.

"You can't go out today, Allie," she said as I fussed with one of the snares.

"I have to."

"Your arm is broken." Her voice was tense. Like she was afraid of what I might do.

"I am aware of that."

"You have a fever." That time it was closer to pleading.

"That is also clear to me." Fuel, Allie. Let the fear burn as fuel. Don't let it overwhelm you.

Why did she need to keep stating the obvious?

"Alastra Hunter, you are in no condition to be the Hunter for this village!"

I looked up to see her fists on her hips, her expression drawn with worry and pain.

"Mother," I tried to be gentle, though it didn't come easy to me. That was Hulanna's strong point. Or at least, it was before she became the bloodthirsty Lady of the Faewald.

I hadn't told my mother about that, and I wasn't going to. That would be one sure way to get her into the Star Stone circle. She'd let my father go help a hurt or afraid Hulanna, but if she realized what Hulanna really needed was a strong scolding, then she'd be the first running into that circle to give it to her.

I tried again. "Mother, this is all my fault. Hulanna. Father. And I really am the Hunter and I have to do this. But I'll take the goats to pasture for you on my way."

"And you'll drink the tea Goodie Herben left for you?" she asked, but her eyes were watery. She was worried. She knew she couldn't stop me – not the way things were out there. And with everything that had happened, it was a wonder she hadn't broken down.

"Yes," I agreed as she took my hair in her hands, unwound it and began to braid it for me again, her hands practiced and quick.

"What's in the cage?" she asked, reaching for the latch when she'd finished braiding.

I gasped and caught her hand.

"Whatever you do," I said. "Don't open it!"

She gave me a puzzled look. "I'll just go get more water to boil your tea, shall I?"

"Thank you," I said gratefully and as soon as she left, I took a little wire and wound it around the latch. If anyone opened this cage, it would be an utter disaster. And yet, I could hardly carry it around with me when I only had one good arm.

Carefully, I carried the cage to the sewing table, set it down beside my mother's kit and pulled my blindfold off.

"Back with us, Hunter?" the Leader asked with a raised eyebrow. His friend wasn't twitching anymore.

Hurriedly, I grabbed a handkerchief and shoved it through the bars of the cage.

"If it burns so much, use this," I said and then I pulled my blindfold off and strode away.

Chapter Twenty-Five

It had not been a good idea to go set snares when I was this feverish. Fortunately, I had brought enough water to keep me hydrated as I hiked through the forest, checking our usual trap lines and setting new snares. So far, I had four coneys in my sack and a brace of marten for furs.

I'd seen four ghouls and I'd sung the song of dispelling and glared at them until they slipped away.

This trap was full, too. A reddish-brown marten with a soft white belly hung from the snare and I couldn't help but run a hand along his fur as I carefully took him from the trap. He was beautiful and deadly. Much like the Fae in my trap back home.

I'd wanted to get one alive when I was a child to keep as a pet, but my father had scolded me.

"Wild things shouldn't be caged, Alastra. They should be free to live and die wild. A cage will hobble their souls and leave them empty haunted things."

We'd never put anything wild in a cage. Our sets killed instantly. Father wouldn't have allowed the suffering or imprisonment of wild and I didn't want it, either.

I swallowed down the memory. My father was likely caged – by the world of Faewald if nothing else – and I was holding three Fae captive at home. Three wild, sentient creatures. I didn't know if the heat I felt wash over me was shame or fever.

I was doing something wrong. Something that went against the way of things. If I wasn't willing to offer them a quick death, I shouldn't be keeping them captive. I rolled my neck to get a kink out and tried not to think about it. I didn't want this decision right now.

I sat down to rest before I reset the snare and gasped.

Between the trees, I could have sworn I saw fire. I blinked and it was gone. Worried, I pulled off my blindfold and nearly re-broke my arm when I scrambled back from what I saw.

A bright, golden, flaming bird rushed over me so close that it almost brushed my face. I recovered from my stumble and ran a few steps trying to keep it in sight. Its marvelous wings were neither feather nor flame, but maybe both. A phoenix – a creature of legend and tale of the Faewald.

I was so intent on its beauty that I crashed into a tree. The pain that flared in my arm wiped away any thought of phoenixes. When I recovered, it was gone.

I slipped the blindfold back on. Maybe I'd imagined it. This fever was not helping things!

I hoped I had imagined it. I didn't want to think about the alternative. Not when I already felt overwhelmed by all this new responsibility.

Irritated at myself and my failing body, I reset my snare and began to work my way back to Skundton. I'd leave these rabbits with Butcher and the marten with Tanner and hopefully, word would get around that Skundton still had a perfectly good hunter, thank you very much.

My mood was dark, despite the tiny successes of the day and the weather seemed to agree, clouds bubbling and roiling in the sky.

I stopped at Chanter's house before I reached Skundton. Marched up the worn wood steps and rapped on the yellow door. There was the sound of scraping chair legs inside and then Goodie Chanter stuck her head out.

"Olen?" I asked.

She shook her head grimly and opened her mouth, but a reedy voice called from within.

"Who is it?"

"Just Hunter, Heldra," Goodie Chanter called back.

"What is *she* doing here?" Heldra asked. I could hear her moving inside the house. I didn't want to deal with her. Not right now.

Hurriedly, I set my gunny sack on the worn step and pulled one of the coneys out. I handed it awkwardly to Goodie Chanter.

"For your dinner," I said.

But Heldra was already sticking her head out the door.

"A measly rabbit? That's all you're here to offer?" She shook her head like she was dealing with a child. She and her mother sure were a lot alike. Separated only by thirty years and twelve children. "You're not welcome here, *Allie*." She wouldn't call me 'Hunter.'

"Can you tell Olen I checked on him?" I asked Goodie Thatcher.

She opened her mouth but once again, Heldra interrupted. "I think you should know that Olen and I are walking out together. He doesn't need to be getting messages from other girls."

"Maybe he does, then," I snapped. "I know if I had you for company, I'd be just dying to hear from almost *anyone* else."

"It's that sharp tongue that keeps any boys from ever thinking about you, Allie Hunter. No one wants to get cut."

The look she shot me was meant to wound, but it was hard not to laugh as I left the house. At least, it was until I remembered what it felt like to hear Olen in the forest with another girl, laughing at me. That other girl had been Heldra. Which meant she was telling the truth.

If you'd asked me yesterday if I cared who Olen Chanter was walking out with, I would have laughed. So why was I crying today?

Fortunately, the roiling clouds finally began to rain and by the time I reached Butcher in Skundton, I was so soaked that no one would ever be able to guess that I'd been crying at all.

Chapter Twenty-Six

I opened the door of the cottage, frustrated to find the fire down to nothing but embers and not a single candle lit. I'd finished my work in town, returned the goats to their pens, and I was head-to-toe in mud and soaked to the skin – not to mention that my arms hurt like anything and my fever was getting worse.

I built up the fire, lit a candle, and set to stripping off my wet clothing. I wasn't easy to do with my broken arm splinted and bandaged. It couldn't bend, and the fingers on that hand were swollen and thick. It needed rest, but I didn't have time to rest it.

I was down to my underthings when my blindfold slipped off as I was tugging my shirt over my head. I bent to recover it and then gasped.

The cage I'd set beside the sewing kit was the only thing I could really see without the blindfold. It still glowed a bright but eerie greenish-blue.

Dripping from the cage out onto the worn wooden floor of our cottage was black tar-like blood. And in the center of the cage, the Fae leader stood with black blood smeared across his clothing, a sewing needle streaked in black in one hand and a growl bubbling up from his throat. Under his feet, lay his fallen comrades, pins and needles scattered in their blood and sticking up from their backs.

"I see I have a pair of new pincushions. What have you been doing while I was gone?" I asked, aghast.

"Slaying my enemies," he said with a fearsome curl to his lip. "What did you expect?"

I leaned down so my face was level with the cage and I could feel my eyes widening as his glamour showed the full effect of perfect immortal features as he sneered at me.

"Not this," I said, swallowing. My heart was sinking. I'd counted on having three of them. Three Fae to put back into the Star Stone circle. One to bring back each of the humans within. I hadn't counted on them killing each other. Fuel, Allie! Use that disappointment as fuel!

My eyes were stinging with frustrated tears despite my reminder as I reached into the cage.

He jabbed my hand with the needle.

"Ouch!"

Again and again. His movements were too quick for me to guess in that strange almost stilted and yet fluid way the Fae had. It was as if they were just jumping over little bits of time and space.

I pulled my hand out as fast as I could, cursing.

"Fine. They can rot in there with you. Enjoy the smell of putrefaction!" I sucked the wounds on my fingers.

"Let me out of the cage," he said grimly. "Let me out and I will not slay you, too."

I snorted. "You're holding a sewing needle. You're going to slay me with that?"

He waggled his eyebrows. "It's not the size that counts."

"Keep telling yourself that," I muttered.

I fumbled through the sewing kit, my hand stinging from where his needle had jabbed it. I could swear it had hit the bones in my fingers.

There it was! I grabbed the stitch-ripper from my mother's kit and struck fast through the bars of the cage, knocking the pin from the Shining One's hands. It flew through the bars and landed on the floor where I snatched it up. The handkerchief was also on the ground, spotted in black blood. I carefully wiped the needle on it and replaced it in my mother's kit.

When I looked up, the Fae had another two needles in both his hands and a ferocious expression on his face.

"I guess this serves me right for setting you down next to something as dangerous as a sewing kit," I said wryly.

"You can't keep me caged forever," he said.

"Can't I?"

A look of horror stole over his face. He didn't know how long this cage would keep him any more than I did. He rallied, posing with one pin point to the floor and the other slung over his shoulder for all the world like a tiny and incredibly attractive child of a god. His open jacket even rippled in an imaginary wind and his tousled hair took on blue glints like raven feathers.

"What's your name?" I asked and he bristled.

He leaned forward as he hissed, "As if I would tell *you*!"

"It's going to be hard to talk to you without a name," I said dryly. "I suppose I could name you. I named the goats that were born this spring after flowers. That seems to fit. You can be 'Daisy.'"

He hissed again.

"Why did you throw the handkerchief out of the cage, Daisy?" I asked. "I thought you wanted to avoid touching the iron bars."

"It fell out in the fight," he said, his chin held up in an arrogant fashion. He was so incredibly pretty like that. Were those the edges of tattoos creeping up his neck? It was hard to tear my eyes off his beauty, even knowing that he was actually nothing like how he seemed and that he'd just slaughtered his two friends and was standing on their corpses. "And now I have no way to guard myself except with the bodies of my slain."

"Mmmhmm," I said, slipping my blindfold on and looking for some dry clothing that wouldn't hurt my arm to put on.

"You're not entirely unattractive without clothing," he commented.

I leaned toward the cage, pulled down the blindfold and growled. "Eyes to yourself, Daisy."

He laughed, a mischievous bitter laugh. "I suppose you may call me Scouvrel."

"Is that your name?"

He sat down on the bodies, cross-legged, resting his twin pins across his lap. "In the Faewald names have power. I could direct your every action with the use of your name. I could bend your will to mine. I could make you my plaything, dancing to my every whim, licking my boots, kissing the soles of my feet."

"Whatever floats your boat," I muttered, fighting with my jerkin and leggings. It was not easy to dress with one hand or with the blindfold only half on so I could keep track of Scouvrel. "You could just lie about your name."

"I can't lie," he said, and the way he said it made it sound like he was either joking or trying to seduce me.

"Does that melt hearts?"

"Does truth excite you?" he returned. "I can make it dance, but I cannot violate it."

I rolled my eyes. "Then I guess you don't know *its* true name."

"Hmmm," he smiled as if that was a novel idea.

"What does Scouvrel mean? Does it have something to do with the scar on your lip?"

I cinched my belt, moved his cage to the floor by the fire and then collapsed on the bearskin rug there. I was cold now and shaking. My arm felt hot. The fever had me in its grip.

"In my world, it's a joke. It means, 'untrustworthy.'"

"I thought you just told me you can't lie."

"Did I?" he asked with a mischievous smirk. "But did I mean 'deceive' or did I mean 'prostrate myself on the ground'?"

"You meant 'deceive,'" I said blearily.

"I've heard it both ways," he said with a smirk, leaning back comfortably as if he were on a silken couch and not finding repose on the corpses of his friends.

I put his cage in my line of sight so I could keep an eye on him without moving. I needed him to stay alive. I needed any knowledge he had about the Fae so I could destroy them.

I closed my eyes – just for a moment – and slipped away.

Chapter Twenty-Seven

"Alastru Livoto Hunter!" my mother's exclamation woke me up. My eyes snapped open.

"I've got your name!" Scouvrel said from inside the cage, his eyes brightening in a way that made me almost want to give him something more just to see them brighten like that again.

I snatched my blindfold down over my eyes again.

"Mother," I groaned. My arm felt heavy – like it weighed a ton. I could hear snickering from the cage. At least someone was having fun.

"What are you doing on the floor? That arm is never going to heal!"

She helped me gently into a chair. "Let's look at that." She examined my arm and felt my head. "You're burning up!"

"Where were you?" I asked, resting my forehead on the table. The room was spinning in a way that made me feel dizzy.

"Checking on things. Calming people down. Making sure that the whole town doesn't light this cottage on fire while we're in it," she said, tightly.

I looked up into her concerned face. "Is it that bad?"

"Worse. We've lost their trust, Allie." She twisted her hands together like she was wringing a cloth.

"But I trapped the Fae that came through the portal," I protested. "I saved Heldra and Denelda! I even saved Olen."

My mother sighed as she got up and filled the kettle. "People don't think like that, Allie. They don't stop to consider your wins. They focus on your failings. And once they decide that you are not of value to them, they take steps. While you and your father fight to protect this family from enemies without, I will keep us safe from enemies within."

"Oh," I said, trying not to look at the cage on the floor by the fire. It wasn't like I'd *meant* to bring enemies within our own home. Not really.

The Fae in the cage snickered.

"It would be best if you could patch things up with Olen," my mother said.

"It would be best if I could open the Star Stone circle and get Father out," I countered.

"One of those is possible," my mother chided as she prepared the healing tea. "And one of those is probably not."

"I agree," I said coyly. "It's nearly impossible to get to Olen with Heldra guarding him like a dog with puppies."

"What if I make a deal with you?" my mother asked.

"Do you make bargains, Little Hunter?" the Fae in the cage whispered, sending thrills up and down my spine as she spoke. I was surprised she couldn't hear him. But maybe it didn't work that way.

"If you go and talk to Olen, I will go and get something for you. Something you need."

"What?" I asked, skeptically. The only things I needed were a healed arm and a way into that stone circle.

"An old book," my mother said. "A hidden one. It holds some of the things our village calls 'old wives' tales' and it may help you find a way to open that circle again. If that's what we really want," she sounded half-hearted.

"Isn't that what you want?" I demanded. "Don't you want Father back? And Hulanna?"

She sighed and when she looked up, her eyes were haunted. "Of course, I do, Allie. But if that means inflicting this town with more loss, can I really choose that path?"

"If you can't, then I'll choose it for you," I said.

She smiled.

"Maybe I'm secretly counting on that," she said as she poured me the healing tea. She frowned. "I am not a very good person."

"Of course, you are, mother," I said, standing to kiss her forehead.

"Drink your tea, Allie," she said primly. "And then go talk to Olen. When you get back, I'll have the book."

I drank my tea and then threw a heavy wool cloak around my shoulders, snatching up the cage and my bow and arrows. The cage I affixed to my belt. It was irritating to walk with it banging against my thigh but better than trying to hold it with only one good arm. I stuffed a pair of fresh handkerchiefs in my pocket, checked my arrows – six good sharp tips – and headed out. My arm felt like the fires of hell had congregated in one spot. I could live with that. If I had to.

"Oh good, we're leaving this hovel," Scouvrel said. "I was longing for some fresh air."

I couldn't see him, but his tone sounded forced.

"Apparently, I can't leave you anywhere on your own or you get into trouble," I muttered as I strode past the goat pen. My mother must have brought them back after I passed out. I should be leading them to pasture again, but I'd agreed to go to Olen's house and to Olen's I would go.

"Trouble is as trouble does."

I took the path through the woods. I could have walked through town, but I didn't want eyes on me. Or ears. Not when I was speaking to a person no one else could see.

"You know I could show you how to open that portal again," Scouvrel said.

"I could just dance like I did last time," I said lightly.

"But was it your dance or your sister's that opened the portal before?" he asked lightly. "The dance only works if you really, really want the Fair Folk to come to your world. Do you really want us in your world Little Hunter?"

"I put you in a cage, didn't I?" I said. "Maybe I do want you all here, so I can cage the rest of your kind."

My words were bold, but inside, fear shot through me. I remembered holding my father's hand as we walked down this very path when I was five years old.

"I'm afraid of monsters, Father," I had said.

"I'm right here with you, Allie. You don't need to be afraid. If a monster comes, I'll kill it."

"What if it kills you?" I had asked in a little voice.

He bent down, pressed his forehead against mine, a hand on either shoulder. Pulling back, he looked me deeply in the eyes and said, "Then you will kill it, Allie. We are hunters, not prey. And we run from no one."

"Little Hunter?" Scouvrel asked, interrupting my memories. "Mortal?"

"Why do you always call me that?" I asked, irritably, my blindfold slipping for just long enough to see him take out a spirit knife in the cage and start trimming his nails. I pulled it back up again before I tripped.

"Because it is what you are. It is what defines a human. That you are mortal. That your years number three score and ten. That you will wither and die in a breath and be gone from this cold world before you've even made a mark. What did you think was the defining characteristic of your humanity?"

Arrogant little creature! He was so sure of his own immortality and invulnerability – even now sitting on a pile of dead comrades.

I gritted my teeth.

It was beings like this who had my father. Who had my sister. What were they doing to test the mortality of the ones I loved? I ground my teeth together, fighting the flare of anger that made me want to smash the cage and the Fae inside it.

"Curiosity," I ground out through my teeth. "That's the defining characteristic of a human. We are so curious that we call up unfathomable monsters just to see if they will come."

He started to laugh. "Ah, but Fae are curious, too. Pick another trait."

"We are vengeful," I said grimly. It wasn't a good choice, but it suited my mood. "Wrong us, and we will make you pay."

He laughed again. "Why do you think Nuuli and Canusu are dead? Even I am a victim of the love of vengeance."

Fortunately, I was almost at the Chanter cottage.

"Best that you stay quiet here," I remarked as I set down the turn in the path to their house. Their goats were also penned when they would have wanted to be at pasture. I felt a twinge of guilt at that. Chanter was gone because of me. And his family suffered for it.

"Or what? You won't harm me, Little Hunter. You need me to get you back through the circle."

I ignored him and knocked on the door.

Chapter Twenty-Eight

"Olen Chanter, you let me in this time, do you hear me?" I knocked on the door a second time. There was still no answer, but there was smoke coming from the chimney. Surely, someone was there!

I glared at the two ghouls watching me from the shadows around the edge of the cottage.

"Boo!"

They fled.

"I don't know why he's avoiding you when you're such a darling to be around," Scouvrel said.

I pulled my blindfold off and fixed him with an angry glare. For a moment his glamor flickered.

"How can you still glamor me when you can't access the rest of your magic?" I asked him.

"Who says I can't?"

I arched my eyebrow. "Would you still be in that cage if you could?"

He frowned, spinning the knife across his knuckles like he was a circus performer. That was quite the trick. I watched him do it again. Could I manage that? I'd look very deadly if I could. Scouvrel certainly did.

"It's a trick of the mind," he said, his voice hesitant.

"Magic," I agreed.

"No, a trick of your mind. I suggest that you should see me this way and if your mind allows it, then it agrees. With humans, it barely takes a suggestion. You love seeing illusions and believing lies. Love it so much, that half the time you make your own glamor. I don't need magic to glamor you. You do it all on your own."

"Maybe instead you should try grooming," I said, sneering at his raggedly, half-washed appearance as the glamor flickered.

"I don't need to groom," he said with a wicked, sharp-toothed smile. "I'm gorgeous."

"That's just the glamor. Underneath it, you stink."

"And you'd still kiss me without stopping until you died of dehydration if I gave you half a chance."

I sniffed, trying to make him believe I was unimpressed. It didn't help that he was right. Whether it was in my head or not, the glamor made me think he was the most desirable creature I'd ever seen.

Enough of this nonsense. I tugged the blindfold back on, knocked again and then opened the door to the Chanter cottage.

"Olen?" I called, glad I couldn't see Scouvrel with the blindfold on. I didn't want him to know any more about me than he already did.

There was a twang of music from the back room. I scraped my boots off carefully and wandered through the house. The fire was built up. A kettle and a pot of soup sat near it on the hearth. The Chanter's cottage looked the same as always. Broken strings, half-full baskets, and cloths that needed folding lay in heaps on any available surface. The place was in desperate need of a good sweeping. But that was how it always was here.

Where was Goodie Chanter?

"Olen?"

His mandolin was so loud he likely didn't hear me.

I opened the door to the back room and found him propped up in bed looking ghastly, the mandolin on his lap and not a stitch of clothing on his torso. A blanket was draped over his waist and down to his bare feet.

He gasped, tugging it up and dropping the mandolin in his lap.

"Oh, I'm so sorry," I said, feeling my face grow hot.

Outside the cabin, I heard the wind pick up, howling down the chimney in an eerie way.

"Allie, what are you doing here?" he sounded horrified.

The snicker from the cage wasn't helping.

"I came to see you."

"In my bedroom?" his voice was a squeak.

"You get your own bedroom?" I asked curiously. There was only one bedroom in our cottage – my parents' bedroom. Hulanna and I had cots in the main room. I looked around curiously at the jerkins and hose flung around the room, the old boots cut up for scrap leather, the scraps of paper with music on them, and the pen and ink set on a stool. Stumps of candle running down the sides of the same stool suggested he liked to read at night. He'd lose his sight that way if he wasn't careful. My brain stuttered over that thought. As if I was one to talk!

"Where's my mother?" he asked.

"That's what I was wondering."

We both looked at each other and my cheeks went from hot to blazing.

"I – " I started at the same time that he said, "You –"

We both fell back into silence and I adjusted my cloak un-necessarily. How did you say, 'I'm sorry for ruining your life, please don't let everyone kill me?'

Awkwardly, I took a bold step to the stool by his bed and sat on it before he could protest. He hugged the blanket around himself even tighter. I untied the cage from my belt and set it on the floor.

"Look," I said. "I'm sorry."

"For what?" he sounded shocked.

"For everything."

He scowled, shaking his head and looking away. "It's not so simple as that Allie."

I waited. I knew Olen Chanter well enough to know that he wasn't done talking. He was waiting to get the words right. He picked up his mandolin and began to strum.

I sighed and my blindfold fell down, the knot loosening and the whole thing sliding right off. I leaned down to pick it up from the floor and gasped when I saw Scouvrel in the cage, his eyes bright as he stared up at Olen, his mouth open in wonder.

He was frozen as if he'd been caught in mid-action. In horror, I saw the tiny body parts strewn around the outside of his cage. He'd been dismembering his fellows and shoving their pieces through the slats of the cage onto Olen's floor. A head was caught in the bars. Swallowing to hold back nausea, I took the end of my staff and used it to pry the head free. I didn't want it bumping against my leg.

Somehow, it was all a little less horrifying in miniature. Or maybe I was getting used to the horror. Maybe it wasn't so bad when it was my enemies.

"Would you stop fiddling, Allie?" Olen asked, an irritated burr to his tone.

I sat up, tying my blindfold back on so I could see him.

"This is all your fault," he said, the music ending abruptly.

"How bad are you hurt?" There was no point in denying it was my fault, but there was nothing that could be done about that now.

"Bad. I can't get out of bed without help. I can't walk the length of the cabin without wanting to collapse. My mother doesn't know what to do. She's hysterical. So's Heldra. A husband isn't much good if he's bedbound."

"He could be," Scouvrel said from floor-level. "You'd be surprised how good that could be."

I kicked his cage.

"Husband?" I asked, feeling like my lips were cold. I licked them. It didn't help at all.

He glowered at me and I didn't know why he was so mad when he said, "We are supposed to get married – or *were* supposed to – or I don't know anymore."

"When?" I felt a hole forming in my gut. I mean, it wasn't like he'd ever hinted at anything like affection to me. He'd just always been friendly. More friendly than anyone else. And I'd begun to hope ... well, hope was too strong a word. To think ... well, even that. I'd started to wonder if maybe, if things were just right, if I turned out to be a *really good* Hunter as I got older, if he might *just maybe* think of me.

"When things were right," he said and sighed. "And now they'll never be right, Allie. My dad is gone forever because of you."

"Why her?"

"Aren't you listening to me?" he snapped. "You took my dad."

"I'm sorry." It felt wrong to even say it. Because it would never be enough.

"Well, who cares if you are," he said viciously. "What good does that do? Does it bring him back?"

"No," I felt like I wanted to cry and that only made me force my tears back and jut my jaw out. I wouldn't cry. Not for him.

Let it fuel you, Allie!

"Does it heal my wounds?"

"No."

"Does it fix my chances with Heldra?" He was getting louder.

"Who cares about Heldra? She's awful!" The words burst out of me. I couldn't hold them back. "She said awful things when Hulanna went through the circle!"

"*I* care about Heldra, Allie! Me. I care about *her* more than I could ever care about *you*. So stop coming here bothering me and go fix this mess you made."

"I can't fix it," I said coldly. Because cold was all I could manage. If I warmed at all, I would start sobbing.

He leaned forward in his bed, coughing as if the movement had hurt his lungs and in his lowest most vicious voice he said, "Try."

I looked at him for a moment with my eyes under the blindfold going wide. He wanted the impossible. Was that really the only thing I could do to fix this?

"The townsfolk want me not to be Hunter anymore," I said numbly. Maybe he'd care about that if he didn't care about anything else.

"Yes, your life is very difficult now that you've ruined mine. You've lost your job," he said dryly and it bit into my heart like an axe chipping a living tree.

I stood up, gathering the cage and my staff and strapping the cage back to my belt.

"And Allie?" Olen said as he picked up his mandolin and began to play again.

"Yes?"

His face was flushed bright red as he looked at me with cold eyes and said, "Don't bother coming back here again without my father. Unless you get him back, I never want to see you again."

I felt my own face flaring hot as I spat back, "Don't worry, Olen. You won't."

It was all I could do not to run out of his cottage, but I kept my dignity and managed a stiff stride, slamming the door as I left.

It would serve him right if Heldra canceled their plans. Heldra! Who would have thought?

It would serve him right if he grew so bitter he couldn't play that stupid mandolin.

It would serve him right if he never saw me again, if I died somewhere in the cold, alone, trying to save his father. I would have succeeded if only I'd had a mandolin player at my side, but instead he ruined his own future by disowning me and turning away.

I felt a hot tear run down my face and in the distance, thunder boomed.

Who was I kidding?

Nothing would serve him right, because this wasn't his fault. It was all my fault. And that made me so angry I wanted to burn all of the Faewald to the ground. I didn't even realize what I was doing until my feet were already on the path to the Star Stone circle.

Chapter Twenty-Nine

When Hulanna had been little, she had always seemed to get her way. If we were walking in the woods as a family, Hulanna would be the one who would drag her feet until our father carried her on his shoulders. If we were in town, Hulanna would be the one who stared longingly at the sweets until our father bought her some.

He'd buy them for me, too, but I knew my parents didn't have the coin for the things I really wanted – my own bow and arrows. Heavy-made hunters boots. Thick woolen clothing to repel any weather. Hulanna's interests had always been more in sweets and ribbons and less in practical things. And it was hard not to envy her the indulgence of Father or the warm smiles of Mother knowing all the time that everyone in the world found her much more charming than I could ever be.

It was just as hard when Hulanna would be invited to stay the night with a friend. Sometimes they would ask me, too, after my mother whispered to the other girls' mothers. And that stung just as badly.

Usually, I would sit at home and press my nose to the window and count ghouls and imagine I was a knight riding a charger and attacking those pathetic shadows.

It had been hard during festivals when Hulanna – with her glossy hair and lovely figure – would be asked by every boy in the village to dance at festivals and no one ever asked me. Except for Olen, but I didn't want to remember that right now.

"I can be useful," I would tell myself. "And when Hulanna causes trouble for the family by making all these boys fall in love with her, I will not cause trouble. I will be sensible and capable of hunting and useful to the family."

But now it turned out that I was no better at being useful than Hulanna had been. Did that mean I had no real value at all? Perhaps Olen had been right. Perhaps, I should open the portal and change places with his father – or mine – or Hulanna. Someone. Anyone. Because any one of them would be a better choice to stay here than Allie Hunter was.

My blindfold slipped off my face and I sat down on a log, catching my breath between rasping coughs and choked sobs. Fury bubbled up under my tears. I hated myself for ruining everything. I hated Olen for noticing it. I hated the town for hurting my mother because of it. I hated the sun for shining and the rain for falling.

I pulled out a handkerchief and wiped my nose with it angrily.

In the cage, Scouvrel stood in the very center, a wild look in his eyes. The bodies were gone, leaving nothing but a streak of blood behind. His glamor flickered on and off. The real him looked almost as frightened as he looked feral.

Was that because he kept bumping up against the iron bars?

"Are the bars hurting you?" I asked him through a thick voice.

"Yes," he said tensely.

"I'd carry you if my arm wasn't in so much pain."

He rolled his eyes. "What if I agree to fix your arm if you agree to give me some respite from the burn of this iron cage?"

"I'm not letting you out," I said, blowing my nose heavily.

"Perish the thought," he said dryly. "How about this – a cloth to protect me from the scorch of the bars. Another needle like I had before. Some thread."

"Sounds like a list for the peddler."

"And in return, I heal your arm."

"It sounds too good to be true," I said. "Which means there's a catch."

"A better bargain would be if you let me negotiate opening the Star Stone circle for you again." He looked hopeful.

"Absolutely not."

He deflated slightly. "But you will bargain for the arm."

"To heal me, you'd have to come out of the cage," I said, warily. "And then you won't go back in. And I will be in real trouble."

"I would like to leave this cage." His expression was hard as a rock.

"I'm not going to negotiate for that," I said stiffly.

"What if I only left for long enough to heal you and I promised to do no further harm to you or any other. And then I immediately went back in? Would that be enough? Would you let me heal you?"

"And the other things?" I asked, trying to be sure I knew what we were bargaining for. "The needle, thread, and cloth?"

"Yes. And one more thing."

"What?"

"A single kiss."

"Just one?"

"Are you saying your kisses are so plentiful that I should buy them by the dozen."

I felt my cheeks heat. The only boy I'd ever dared think of a future with just told me I'd never see him again.

"Thinking of the music boy?" he asked, tilting his head to the side with interest.

"None of your business."

"The boy who played that delightful instrument – the instrument with the swirling body like a stolen wind?" His eyes were bright and deep as he spoke.

"Are you in love?" I asked, shocked.

"Absolutely!" he sighed.

"Really?" I squinted at him.

I didn't know –

I hadn't thought –

He laughed. "With the mandolin. That's what you called it, right? Mandolin?"

Oh.

"Yes," I agreed hurriedly as he smirked at me.

"Jealous?"

"Of a mandolin?" I kept my tone dry. Was I jealous? Of the affection of a Fae? How ridiculous!

He laughed musically. "Think about the bargain. You'd have a working arm."

I felt my cheeks grow hot. And he would be the first boy I'd ever kiss. If he was even a boy.

"Why a kiss?" I demanded.

"Why not?" He shrugged.

I stood up suddenly, pulled the blindfold up over my eyes and tried to ignore the musical laughter from the cage.

Chapter Thirty

It took ages to start a fire in the rain. I almost didn't manage it and I probably wouldn't have if I hadn't started before it really started pouring. So now I was huddled over a poor excuse for a fire in the lee of one of the Star Stones, listening to Scouvrel's scornful comments as I tried to keep the fire going while ignoring the pain in my arm.

My head was pounding, little spikes of pain seemed to drive through my eyes intermittently. It was better if I left the blindfold on, but every so often I slipped it off and looked around. I could easily be caught unawares here by the stones – and that would spell disaster.

"If you don't want to make a bargain with me, why are we here?"

"Someone should be guarding the doorway," I snapped. Not that I could even draw that bow right now. "And there's no one else but me."

"Are you thinking of giving yourself for the boy's father?" he asked, sounding genuinely curious.

I didn't answer. I was thinking of it. I'd been thinking of it ever since Olen told me not to come back without him.

"You're worth more than the Chanter is." Scouvrel hesitated. "I think. I haven't heard him sing. That mandolin was a thing of heaven and hell mixed in a melody that scorches furrows into the heart."

Adoration rippled through his voice. I'd kill to have a man love me like that.

Now, where did that thought come from?

"Yes, I noticed you fell pretty hard for it," I said. I could see why the poem suggested that music blinded them. He was as useless as a love-sick puppy where music was concerned.

"I would pay in rubies and moonstones to hear it again."

I laughed at the doleful longing in his voice.

"You find me amusing?" It seemed that his scorned pride could sting as badly as mine did.

I cleared my throat. "Not at all."

I could still lie, even if he couldn't. I added more fuel to the fire, freezing when I heard a twig snap. I was on my feet in a heartbeat, staff held out, ready to strike. My arm sang a song of pain and misery.

"Allie? Are you here?"

I breathed a sigh of relief. It was only my mother.

She emerged from the tangled shadows and trees with a large pack on her back, a kettle in one hand, and long poles in the other.

"I thought I would find you here," she said gently. "You're a mess. An open field in a rainstorm is no place for a girl with a broken arm."

"It seems to be the only place these days," I said, not able to keep the bitterness from my words

"I take it things with Olen went poorly?" she set the kettle on the ring of stones I made around the fire, kicking one of the stones out of the circle. "Circles aren't safe here, Allie. Don't make them if you don't have to."

"Olen never wants to see me again."

"I'm sure that's not true," she said, setting the pack beside me in the lee of the stone and pulling a square of canvas out of the top of the pack. "No, stay sitting. You look awful. No point in getting a fever on top of a broken bone. Drink the tea when it gets hot."

I felt my face go hot. I didn't like lying to her about my health, but if I admitted that I already had a fever she might try to keep me at home.

"Is that a tent?" I asked.

"I know better than to try to keep you home," she said with a shake of her head. "You're just like your father. He would have been insisting on staying up here, too – just to keep track of that circle. And he would pretend he was only going to be a few hours and then the night would pass and then another and then I'd give up and set up a tent for him. So, I've learned my lesson. I won't hear your lies. I'll just put the tent up myself."

"Thank you," I said meekly. It was hard to be angry in the face of this aggressive level of kindness.

"There's food in the bag and there's a sewing kit to fix your clothes, a sachet of healing tea, blankets, a pot, and a water bottle. And dry clothes, which is lucky since you're soaked through." She already had the tent nearly set up. She pounded a stake with a mallet and moved to the other side of the tent pounding the next stake. "It's probably useless to tell you to get some rest and drink your tea and keep that arm dry, but I'm telling it to you anyway."

"I will," I said in a small voice.

She cinched the ropes affixed to the corners of the canvas, tying them off efficiently as if she did this every day.

"Don't look so surprised. Before you were born, I did this with your father almost every weekend. You don't think I was born old, do you?"

"Everyone hates me," I said through thick lips.

She paused. "You know I don't hate you, Allie."

"You don't count," I said.

She shook her head. "You think so now, but someday you'll realize that parents do count. We count for a lot. I will have your back down there," she gestured to the town. "While you do what you must up here. But. I want a promise from you."

"What promise?" I felt like I was going to cry. It was worse having her love me and care than it had been without the love. It was like her very kindness highlighted all the reasons that everything else hurt so much.

"Promise you won't throw your life away to try to fix things."

I stayed quiet. I hadn't decided whether I was going to do that or not.

She shook her head, making an irritated sound in the back of her throat. She jammed the mallet into the bag she'd brought and pulled out a battered little leather-bound book.

"You will need to read this," she said. "It's the book I was telling you about. Goodie Herben would be mad as a goat with one horn if she realized I took it, but you need it." She looked up at the sky. "Do you know what it means to be Hunter?"

I disguised my surprise at the abrupt change in conversation by pouring the tea into a battered metal mug she'd brought.

"It means I hunt predators and enemies for the town."

"And?"

I shook my head. "And what?"

"You have to hunt *every* enemy or predator, or you stop being Hunter," she said.

"Okay."

She looked uncomfortable. "It's your father who should be telling you this."

"What?"

She hadn't looked this uncomfortable when she'd told Hulanna and me about the birds and the bees.

"It means you have to hunt everything. If a phoenix, say, were in our land, you would *have* to hunt it. You couldn't just let it fly by."

"Oh." That was going to be a problem. "Do I have to catch it or just hunt it?"

She gave me a long look. "The Hunter has a unique relationship with the land. You have to hunt it if it needs hunting. You have to kill it if it needs killing. And you have to refrain if it doesn't."

I felt like there should be more to that explanation. That was just basic herd management.

"You'll see," she said significantly. "Besides, you're also a girl."

I bridled. "So are you. Are you suggesting girls can't be Hunters?"

She smiled wryly. "Of course, you'd take it that way. No, Allie, I'm saying that as a woman you already have a connection to the land and that might make this whole Hunter thing more powerful. Especially since you found that cage." She nodded to the Cage of Souls. I felt the urge to tug my blindfold off and see why Scouvrel was so quiet, but I resisted. "You might be a lot more connected than your father was. You might be Oolag."

That, I had never heard of before, though I heard Scouvrel gasp quietly in his cage.

"What does that mean?"

She looked at the thunder clouds in the sky above us with an uncomfortable expression. "Read the book. It will help. I'll be back tomorrow with more food. And for heaven's sake, get some sleep."

She hugged me so suddenly and fiercely that I almost dropped my tea, my bad arm flaring with pain and then she was gone, striding through the wet grass, her skirts soaked to the knee, without so much as looking back.

Well.

We all dealt with insanity in our own way, I supposed.

I gripped the book and decided maybe I should read it before I spoke to her about this again.

Chapter Thirty-One

The night that the forest ghouls grew far too plentiful, I was eight. Chanter stopped by our house in a panic. They'd driven him from the mountain plains.

"Hundreds," he'd said. "They poured down from the north like living shadows."

He'd left as quickly as he came, jumping at every shadow.

"I need Allie tonight," my father had said when he left.

My mother's face was haunted as she grabbed my hand, clutching it to her breast.

"It will be okay, love," my father said to her. "But I can't do this alone. I need Allie."

"Maybe I can –" my mother had started by his headshake was enough to stop her.

"No, love. I need Allie. She's good with the bow and small enough to put in a tree while I herd them to her."

I felt pride shoot through me, but my mother looked in my eyes with worry. "Don't shoot your father by accident, Allie."

"I won't." I was already pulling on my forest leathers as my father readied my small bow and checked over the arrows.

"Don't fall out of the tree," my mother reminded me.

"I won't."

"Don't –"

"She knows, love," my father said and in a flurry of activity and wind we were out of the house and before I knew it, he was tying me to a branch against a thick tree.

"Keep an arrow nocked but not drawn. I'll kill those I can, but you be sharp. When I drive them past your tree, take any shot you can. Even if it isn't good. They took ten goats last night. And that was before they terrified Chanter. They're getting too plentiful. And rumors from the south say that if we can't contain them, a squad of the Knights of Light will be sent here."

"And we don't want that?" I asked, nervously.

"Best to keep from the eyes of the powerful, Little Hunter. The powerful only bring trouble on their heels and fire in their wake. Five days here and they could leave a generation of trouble when they go. A month? Well, we'd never have the same town again. Ready now?"

I nodded and he ghosted out into the trees. Someday, I would be able to sneak like that. Someday I would be as skilled and good as my father.

I kept my arrow nocked and my attention focused.

I kept my thoughts on the task at hand. I could do this. I'd been learning. I was ready.

When the ghouls came, I shot every arrow I had, until my arms felt like dead lumps. It was a long time until my father returned and I was so proud when he came to untie me with a huge grin and green ghoul blood all over his hands and splashed on his clothes.

"How many?" I'd asked breathlessly.

"You shot twelve," he said. "I took down another thirty."

"Is that enough?"

"For now, Little Hunter, for now."

"I want to be the greatest Hunter ever," I said sleepily.

"I will teach you to live in the cold and scarcity and come out alive and strong," he whispered as he carried me home. "I will teach you that fear and anger are fuels to use. I will teach you to hunt."

I never heard what plans he had for Hulanna. He must have whispered them to her when I was not around.

Chapter Thirty-Two

When my mother was gone, I reached into the pack and found the sewing kit and the spare rope. The rope, I wound into a sling. My splinted arm was blindingly painful, healing tea or no, and I hoped that tying it to my body might ease some of that pain.

When I was done, I tugged my blindfold off and looked at Scouvrel.

"How do I open the portal?" I asked him, narrowing my eyes.

He smiled. "Bargain with me and I'll tell you."

I hesitated. He'd already offered me one bargain – this sewing kit, cloth, and a kiss in exchange for healing.

"Are you considering the other bargain I offered?" His eyes lit up.

I looked away. I was considering it. But could I phrase the bargain in a way that would force him to stay in the cage?

"I feel the circle is weak," he said in a low, seductive voice and when I glanced back at him, his eyes met mine and his smile turned alluring. It was easy to forget that his glamor wasn't real. "I feel the creatures on the other side who wish to come through. Some already have. Can you hunt with one arm? Can you trap with one hand? Those snares you set were difficult and even now your head is hot with the pain. Make the bargain with me and you will have two arms with which to hunt."

"If you can heal my arm, you can heal my sight," I said. "Maybe I'll bargain for that."

If I was going to bargain with him, I should try to get the best deal possible.

He laughed. "I don't think I want to bargain for that. I like playing with my food and if you can't see me in here, then the fun ends."

"What good are you if you can only go halfway?" I asked, pulling the thimble from the sewing kit and filling it with tea for him. "Here. Enjoy. Maybe it will heal something in you."

He looked at me warily.

"What?" I asked.

"What is the catch? What do you want for the tea?"

"Your undying friendship," I said snidely, shoving it through the bars. The pain was making me cranky. I replaced my blindfold, opened the book, and scooted closer to my smoldering fire.

"Done," he said, with a twist to his voice that made me think he was getting cranky, too.

I began to read. It was a journal, of sorts. But not a daily thing. Sometimes the entries were days apart but just as often there were gaps of months or years between entries. And as the book went on, the handwriting and ink changed many times. So, a journal but kept by more than one person. I flipped through, trying to count how many people had owned this journal, but I lost track after a dozen, distracted by what was written in the book. I stopped in the center, reading a few lines jotted in a spiky black hand.

We hid the key carefully for our daughters and we pray it is found by none but them. To open the circle is to birth into the world horrors beyond imagining. The world with ache with the pain of it as a woman in the pains of labor. But sometimes even labor is necessary.

And then another entry:

In a ring but deep you go
In a spot the wind won't blow
Buried deep but not in dirt
Hold your breath with death you flirt.

And that was it. It reminded me of when Hulanna had hidden her coins – and mine – in a place she called, "very, very safe" and then promptly forgot where it was. We'd spent the entire Spring looking for them until I finally found them one morning in a robin's nest under the eaves of our shed. I'd scolded her and she'd laughed.

"Well, they were safe, weren't they?" she'd said back.

These ancestors of ours seemed to have the same approach to keeping things safe.

I flipped the pages until I found another interesting list. It was a list of rules for the Faewald:

Rules of the Faewald:

1. *One goes in and one comes out*
2. *Fae may not lie. If a mortal lies to Fae, a price will be paid.*
3. *Do not eat or drink their food without adding salt*
4. *Everything is a bargain*
5. *None may tamper with a fated match*
6. *There is to be no singing or music in the Faewald*
7. *There may be no iron in the Faewald*
8. *None may interfere with a game*

There was a squeal beside me, and I startled, ripping off the blindfold and losing my place in the book.

"What are you doing?" I yelled, leaping back from where a mouse twitched and twisted on the ground beside the cage.

Scouvrel had broken the creature's neck.

"It was going to kill me," he said calmly.

"The mouse was." My tone was dry as a tomb.

"Of course. They hate me."

"It's a mouse. It doesn't hate you," I peered at the mouse. Its ears were small and it's tail stubby. This kind of mouse lived in the tall grass on these high plains.

"It hates me – as all mortal creatures do – because it knows I want to eat it."

"You want to eat mice." I kept my tone dry as dust. He was just trying to get me to react because he loved the drama. I could almost see the twinkle in his eye. "Are you part owl?"

"I want to eat everything." His grin was predatory. "I want to eat the whole world like a wheel of cheese. Feel it crumble under my tongue and melt in my mouth."

"Eating that much cheese will just make you sick," I said, but a thrill of fear shot through me.

It was easy to forget what Scouvrel was when he was in a cage and made small. Easy to forget that he was dangerous and deadly. He'd kill a mouse just for scurrying by. He'd kill me if he could. I should be very careful if I planned to bargain with him. I should make sure that I had thought of everything.

The rain had settled into a dull drizzle as the sun began to set. I read until I could read no more.

I built up my fire, gathered enough wood for later and brought out the food my mother had packed. Goat cheese and bread. I smeared the cheese on the bread and broke off a small piece for Scouvrel, pulled down my blindfold and offered it to him gingerly.

"In lieu of the world, perhaps you'll settle for goat cheese."

"In exchange for what?" he asked warily.

I shook my head. Not everything needed to be a bargain, did it?

"Oh, I don't know," I said irritably. "When I'm hungry, you can feed me. Fair enough?" He hesitated for long enough that I laughed. "Too much to ask? And here I thought Fae were brave and bold."

"Boldness has nothing to do with it. If I agree to that, I can never let you starve to death." His voice was velvet smooth for someone utterly at my mercy.

I leaned in close – being careful not to get within range of his grip. I'd learned a good lesson from the mouse.

"I think you mistake how much power you have, little Faerie. You are the one in *my* cage."

He rolled his eyes. "Life can be a trickster. Today I am your captive. Perhaps tomorrow you will be mine. Best to think for the future, or the past will eat your bones."

I wanted to come up with a smart reply but at that moment a wind tore across the field, whipping my fire up into a frenzy. With a cry, I leapt to my feet, beating the fire back with careful stomps. A sound like a blowing horn pierced the air.

Chapter Thirty-Three

I'd forgotten to pull my blindfold back up.

How had I still seen the fire with only my spirit eyes? But it was still there, burning brightly beside Scouvrel's cage. And all around us, in the howling dark of the night, alive now with calls and screams, faerie creatures poured from the Star Stone circle, running, galloping or flying at full speed.

A creature like a milky-bright horse with a massive horn jutting from its brow sailed toward me and I flung myself to the ground, screeching in pain as my broken arm took the brunt of my fall. I scrambled – blindly – for my staff and came up with a piece of firewood, my heart hammering in my chest.

The unicorn had gone, disappeared from sight and vanishing in every direction were silvery hinds, cat-owl crosses, fluttering creatures of fangs and scraps of wing that I didn't recognize and pouncing, leaping creatures of claws and death.

I watched them leave with a sinking heart. There had been dozens. Dozens of faerie creatures that I would now be responsible for as a Hunter. And there was just no way I could keep Skundton safe from all of them.

I cursed as Scouvrel broke into laughter.

"You won't catch any of them with that broken arm."

I didn't even know where I would start if I had two good arms. I'd only brought a dozen arrows with me.

"Bargain with me," Scouvrel cooed. My heart melted to soft taffy at the sound. I fought against that warmth, with little success.

With a grunt, I sat down heavily beside his cage and tried to compose my thoughts. There were no other options now. This was a problem that only I could solve, and I needed both arms to solve it.

I would have to phrase my bargain carefully.

"I will give you," I began, watching him stand up excitedly on the tips of his toes, his eyes brightening at my words, his smoke-wings springing to life behind him. "The sewing kit and a cloth. The pin and a kiss – as promised." I tried not to shudder at the thought of kissing him, knowing what he was – or to be too eager knowing how he looked in all his glamor. "If you –"

I hesitated.

"Go on," he whispered rapturously. He looked at me like he had looked at the mandolin when Olen played it.

"If you," I cleared my throat. "Heal my arm and do not harm me or try to kill me in any other way, make no attempt to escape, or call someone else to help you escape while you are out of the cage, or force me to help you escape, no attempt to kill yourself or any other thing while you are out of the cage, or attempt to destroy the cage, flee through the portal or otherwise keep yourself from returning to the cage and that you will immediately return to the cage and your captivity as soon as my arm is healed without looking for a loophole or other way to avoid your fate."

He laughed. "I think I will like playing with you, Alastru. You are good at devising games."

I felt a chill run down my spine.

"I accept your bargain," he said with a wide grin. "You have to say, 'We are agreed.'"

"We are agreed."

I could feel the cold sweat forming on my brow and between my shoulder blades as I swallowed and steeled myself to open the cage.

"A bargain is a bargain," he reminded me, smiling wickedly as if he had a secret. Maybe he did.

I carefully unwound the wire as his lips parted and his mouth opened with anticipation.

I swung open the door of the cage and let him out.

He burst through the door like a whirlwind, moving from tiny and spiritual to suddenly full-sized and as tangible as I was. His black smoke wings swirled around him and the wicked glint in his grass-green eyes made my heart race.

He was wickedness made flesh, temptation in physical form, destruction embodied. My heart fluttered traitorously. Like the foolish moth it wanted to draw so close to the flame that its wings would conflagrate.

He was taller than me. I'd forgotten that.

And he stood so close that I had to look up to see his face.

His smile, twisted and devastating, grew as he looked me up and down and he bit his lip when his eyes met my breast where my heart and lungs betrayed my emotions. I forced my face into stillness.

"Anxious, Little Hunter?" he crooned.

"No more than you are, little Fae," I replied, trying to be glib but not able to fully disguise the hitch in my voice.

"Alastru Livoto Hunter," he said my name in perfect diction. "Go into the tent and wait for me."

I laughed. "Taking liberties already?"

His eyes opened in stunned awareness. "Your name – is that not your name?"

"Of course, it is," I replied smiling cynically. "You heard my mother say it."

"But it doesn't work," he looked appalled.

"Work? It tells me you're talking to me. What else did you think it would do?"

"It's your name?" He asked again, stepping forward so his forehead nearly touched mine. His smoky wings swirled around me, too. I shifted my weight like a rabbit wondering which way to dart. "Your true name?"

"Yes," I said, keeping a tight reign on my tone. I hadn't bet on him being so ... irresistible. So powerful. So utterly unyielding. I'd let him free without remembering quite how powerful he was. And now I wasn't sure if I could hold him to his bargain. If I could get him back inside that cage.

Part of me wondered if I even should. Was it right to cage a living thing like this one? But I'd seen what he did to the other Fae in the cage. And they had been wounded. I'd seen what he did to the mouse.

His face was mere inches from mine as he leaned down to look in my eyes with his brilliant green gaze. I squeaked like a mouse.

He laughed a rich wine-and-velvet laugh.

"Bargain," I gasped. "Keep to the bargain."

"Oh, I will," he said, his smile turning taunting. "Are you afraid of me, Little Hunter? Or do you desire me? Are you longing for that kiss?"

He drew out the word "kiss" until every nerve in my body seemed to stand on end. He wasn't wrong about that.

"I've seen your true nature," I reminded him – and myself.

He *tsked*. "This is my true nature."

"You said you would heal my arm."

His grin deepened. "Yes, Little Hunter, but I didn't say when."

I could feel the blood draining from my face, but he laughed again and shook his head.

Gently, he took my arm in both hands, unwinding the bandage wrapped around the splint. I flinched from the flare of pain, gritting my teeth together as it burned hot.

"I thought it was one for one," I said through gritted teeth, trying to think of anything other than this pain. "How did all those beasts get through?"

'One for one for humans and Fae," he said lightly. "The Fae creatures serve the Fae. They are not bound by the same rules."

Which meant they could send as many of them as they wanted. And I would have to hunt them all.

"Your sister likely knows you well enough to know what an influx of beasts would do to your concentration," he said, lifting his eyebrows like this was somehow funny. The blue-green light that glowed from him in my spirit-vision picked out every feature in perfect detail as he pulled the splint from my arm and clicked his tongue at the swelling. He touched the skin and I bit back a cry as he hissed. "It's hot. It's likely worse than you thought."

"What does my sister have to do with the Faerie beasts?" I asked, fighting back tears of pain.

"She sent us here, didn't she?" he said, glancing up to my eyes as if testing what I knew. "The other two were of her court. And I was a prisoner. Three Fae to catch one mortal girl. It should have been easy enough."

"Why would she send a prisoner?" I asked.

"Maybe she thought you would kill me."

"Then why send the other two? I presume they were allies of hers since you killed them."

"Maybe she doesn't care who dies."

"That doesn't sound like her."

"Maybe it would if you knew her better."

I scowled, frustrated by might-have-beens, but my scowl washed away as pain burst through my arm, blinding all my senses, filling me up with agony. I wanted to scream, to cry, to run.

After what felt like a long time, the pain fled like an injured doe. I blinked and saw him standing there in front of me, still holding my arm, his head tilted to one side.

"What was that?" I gasped.

"The price. Magic isn't free."

"I thought the price was a sewing kit and a kiss!" I said, feeling my face grow hot with something other than shame, my body tingle with the desperate urge to hit him.

He laughed. "That was the price for my help. Magic takes its own price. In this case, it sped up the healing. You experienced weeks of pain in a moment. A good trade, don't you think?"

This. This was what made the Fair Folk dangerous, I realized as I swallowed back bile. The deals they thought were 'good' were brutal and vicious things.

I refused to answer him, refused to show weakness. Instead, I tested my arm, moving it every which way to check that it was healed correctly. To my surprise, glowing green light in the shape of thorns twisted around both of my arms. I gasped.

"What did you do to me?"

"Still not me. You really don't know about the price of magic?"

I glared at him.

I could tell he was suppressing laughter when he said, "The first touch of magic leaves a residue. In keeping with your nature. This residue tells me that you will be prickly and liable to draw blood."

"Let me guess," I said, nearly spitting the words. "Your first brush with magic left serpents."

He laughed and showed me his arms and for the first time, I realized that what I'd thought were tattoos were actually inky patterns of darkness, almost like non-light. They were in the shape of stylized feathers.

"You're the thorns, Hunter. I'm light as a feather."

I rolled my eyes to his laughter. "This is funny to you."

"Like you wouldn't believe." His eyes widened innocently, and his smile became angelic. "And isn't it convenient that my entertainment has healed you?"

I couldn't deny that, so I didn't try. "You said you'd go back in the cage the moment you were done."

"I'm waiting for my payment," he said, and now his eyes had a wild edge to them that made me nervous. My heart sped up. "I see you are equally eager."

I licked my lips. The kiss. He meant the kiss.

I couldn't forget the look of him without his glamor – the feral look in his eyes, the tangled matted hair, the pointed teeth and blood-soaked hands and the scraps of flesh hanging from his skeletal wings.

And I couldn't stop looking at the glamored nature of him now – perfect in every way. Perfectly evil.

And I didn't know if I was horrified or excited. If I desperately wanted out of the bargain or if I wished he'd bargained for more.

I could almost taste what he would taste like, could almost feel the touch of his lips already. Would he bite? Would I care?

He released my healed arm and stepped in close, leaning his forehead against mine.

My heart hammered a staccato rhythm.

"If there's no kiss, there's no getting back in the cage," he whispered.

I could will him back in.

"I won't be so easy to trap twice."

I turned my face up to his, accepting and afraid all at once. I wasn't sure if he kissed me or if I kissed him. It was no gentle meeting of the lips. It was not the sweet summer kiss of lovers. His kiss was violent and insistent crushing my lips against his as his hands grabbed my waist and pulled me toward him. He felt – hungry – as if he really did want to eat the whole world.

And I was hungry, too.

It took every ounce of will inside me to stop. To stop kissing him, tasting him, wanting him.

As soon as my senses cleared, I shoved him away as hard as I could. The look of triumph on his face was devastating.

"Bargain complete," I said breathlessly.

The triumph vanished, replaced by vulnerability and desperation and then he vanished.

Only he didn't vanish. He was back in the cage in miniature form and the look on his face was of violent rage and bitter disappointment.

I felt the exact same way.

Quickly, I jammed my blindfold down so that I wouldn't have to look at him. I didn't want to imagine a different outcome. I didn't want to see his desperate desire for what I wouldn't' give him. I wound the wire over the door to fasten it shut, grabbed the sewing kit and cloth and shoved them into the cage. There. My part was done. I didn't take the blindfold off – didn't dare.

But I did whisper to him, "You are the worst kisser I've ever experienced."

"I'd be willing to lay ten crowns that I'm the only kisser you've ever experienced," he said lightly, but the tug of compassion in my gut told me his light tone disguised hidden swells of pain.

What was I thinking, feeling bad for a Shining One? I was ten-times the fool for that sentiment.

I knew one thing for sure. I was never going to let him out of that cage again. Not when he had so much power. And such a devastating ability to use it.

Chapter Thirty-Four

My chest was heavy as I fastened the cage to my belt again. I'd promised before that I would carry it if I had two good arms, but I needed my arms for the bow. I kicked dirt over the fire but left the rest of my camp set up. If all went well, I would be back tonight to guard the village from the Star Stone circle. I'd need all my supplies then. After a moment's consideration, I tucked the extra wood under the tent. It would be easier to start a fire with dry wood – though the rain seemed to be over now.

Bright stars speckled the crystal clear sky as I strode out over the long grass, the bow in my hand. Finally being free of pain gave me a feeling of lightness and optimism I hadn't felt in days. It was a strange thing to realize how heavily the pain had held me down – like a great weight on my back.

I shied away from the knowledge that something else weighed on me now. Guilt. Not just guilt for the fates of Father, Chanter, Olen and Hulanna – all my fault – but guilt for Scouvrel's fate, too. Try as I might, I couldn't reach through the tangle of my own emotions to know whether I felt guilty for trapping him or setting him free. For kissing him at all – or for liking it. And I hated myself for the guilt. And hated myself worse because I couldn't decide if I should be even more guilty.

I let that anger propel me down the forest path. Fuel, Allie! Don't drown. Let it fuel you.

I was going to have to take the blindfold off. I hadn't thought to bring a light and though the stars were bright over the high plains, their light didn't penetrate the forest. I was going to be stumbling around blindly whether I did that in the spirit realm or the real world. I made a huffing sound as I tried to see in the faint light. I didn't want to pull the blindfold off. I didn't want to confront what Scouvrel might say or do.

I ran a hand over my hair and looked at my hand – surprised that there were no dark green thorny vines on it. The tattoo that the magic had left must only be visible in the spirit world. I clenched my teeth. I hated that it had left a mark on me. Hated even more that Scouvrel had let it do that without warning me. All this hate was going to take a toll on me.

But a few steps down the path, I stumbled into a tree and had to stop. I was going to have to take the blindfold off. Reluctantly, I pulled it down and let my eyes readjust to the spirit world. There were the glowing green tattoos. I shivered at the sight of them proclaiming to any Fae who might glance in my direction that I was thorny and difficult. So what? Would it be better to be delicate and easily crushed like the flower? Like Hulanna? I thought I might be ill.

The paths of the faerie creatures scorched trails across the woods. Scouvrel's cage glowed brightly in their midst and in the middle of it, he was dutifully scrubbing himself with a bit of the cloth and the thimble of water.

I ignored the process. He had very little modesty.

"Trying to decide which creature to trap and kill?" he asked with a playful lilt to his voice. "For a price, I could tell you."

"No more bargains," I muttered.

"Don't you enjoy my games?"

"I don't play games," I huffed.

"Oh, I think you do. I think you weave games like a spider weaves a web and you don't even know you're doing it. How charming."

The flying creatures had been small. I could probably save them for later. I was more concerned about the land creatures – the ones who had clearly been predators. Them and the unicorn. Horses were bad-tempered enough. One with a horn could only be worse.

I bit my lip and tried to decide which of the glowing spirit trails might be his. What made me think of a unicorn?

"Feeling that sore about the tattoo?" Scouvrel asked innocently. "It almost suits you."

"I can live with the tattoo," I countered, choosing a bright purple trail. That one made me think of a unicorn. It felt – powerful, unpredictable, a little insane. "It's the kiss that really turned my stomach."

He laughed like I'd told a good joke. I ignored him and followed the trail, going slowly so I didn't trip over fallen logs and stumps. I could avoid trees by sticking to the trail – the unicorn couldn't go through living trees either, but he stepped easily over fallen tangled trees that took me long minutes to navigate.

"You've chosen the unicorn," Scouvrel said, feigning interest. "You *do* know they are cursed?"

"Yes, I'm the curse," I muttered. I was making slow time. If the faerie creature was out to do damage, it easily could.

"If you kill a unicorn you have to pay the head fee."

"What's a head fee?" I asked, if only to try to distract me from the fear I felt at the idea of shooting the creature I'd seen. It was huge and magnificent. Beautiful. Should I really kill something like that?

"Different unicorns belong to different Courts," Scouvrel said, his voice slightly muffled like he had something over his head. I did not look. It wasn't my business what he was doing with what he'd bargained for himself. "Kill one, and you must pay the Court the fee they set."

"Like a tax?"

"Certainly," he agreed. "But they might not ask for coins. It might be a tax of days. Or the use of one of your hands. Or that delightful sense of humor of yours. You'd be awfully dull without it."

"Yes, that's my greatest fear," I said, climbing over a tangle of trees. "Being dull."

"It's like hell," Scouvrel said, but then paused. "Not that I would know. I am never dull."

"Mmmhmm," I said, but I wasn't listening. I could hear something now. A scuffling sound and then a muffled scream.

I hurried up, going as fast as I could without tripping. The purple trail was brighter now as it wove through the ghostly, unformed spirit-version of the forest.

I saw the dead man before anything else.

He was nothing but an unfocused, warbling ghost of an impression, as if his spirit had left nothing but a whisper behind.

Above him, the Unicorn stood, proud and tall, horn raised in the air. It glittered like a thousand stars were sweeping up off its skin like steam might lift off a real horse. It stood on its back legs, pawing the air and snorting, it's spirit form raw, sharp, and angular – as if a wolf had been reborn as a horse.

Terror turned my mouth dry and made my heart trip over itself. It was so big. And it was right here.

It had already killed someone. Maybe. Unless that man was somehow dead before the unicorn arrived.

I checked the string of my bow, my eyes still fixed on the scene before me.

A man's whimper caught my attention and that's when I saw a second man – this one in the tree above the unicorn. But the tree he had climbed could not support his weight and he dangled from the bending willow, his back bare inches from the unicorn's horn when the unicorn stood and pawed the air. The willow wouldn't hold long. It would break under the strain.

I swallowed, drew an arrow from my quiver and felt along the fletching to be sure it was undamaged.

I would have one shot at this. One shot or the unicorn would wind me.

I forgot everything else except for me and my prey. Carefully, quietly, I adjusted my stance and nocked the arrow. I slipped my blindfold half on and half off. It made me feel queasy, but I'd done this before. I could do it again.

It would have to be a standing shot. Moving to prone right now would draw attention. I drew the bow, my arms aching at the pressure, but fortunately, my newly healed arm was strong enough for the draw. I brought the string back until the knot in it touched my nose in the exact right place.

The unicorn froze, it's blazing eyes staring right at me. It had seen me draw.

One chance at this.

My heart was hammering. I chose my placement. The unicorn was angled slightly away from me. Not perfect, but good enough. I would put the arrow right behind his shoulder.

One chance.

I fought the queasiness of my double vision, swallowed, and loosed the arrow.

"Boo!" Scouvrel said.

The unicorn leapt at the sound of his voice.

I heard my own curse at the same time that the arrow struck – too far back. I couldn't see where it had hit but I thought it might be the hip.

I cursed again as he leapt toward the trees, my fingers fumbling for a second arrow.

"Why did you do that?" I demanded, glancing at Scouvrel through my double vision. I had to swallow back nausea but he only crossed his arms over his chest triumphantly, his glamor flickering to show a much cleaner, neater, but no less wild Fae under his assumed beauty.

"Hunter?" a quavering voice asked from the tree. "Is that you?"

Chapter Thirty-Five

The only way it could have gone worse was if I had shot Fletcher instead of the unicorn. And even that might not have really been worse.

"Are you going to come down from that tree?" I asked roughly, pulling my blindfold up so I could look at the dead man below him.

"With that winning personality, it's a wonder you haven't found a mate," Scouvrel said but I ignored him. I'd heard that before. More times than I could count and from people who could wound me more than he could.

The dead man was Woodreaver. By the gouge in his chest – wider than my fist – I guessed he'd died immediately, but it still didn't stop the bile from rising in my throat or the burning feeling in bowels that suggested I was going to be sick if I couldn't pull myself together.

I'd been dealing with dead animals all my life from the time I was a toddler sitting with my dad while he cleaned partridges, opening up their crops so I could see the leaves and pine buds they ate, to the time I was seven and he gave me my first marten to skin and clean with the words, "Do a good job and you can have the coin from the skin for yourself."

But I had no experience with dead people. It wasn't the same – not even close. There was something horrifyingly wrong about seeing Woodreaver – who I'd known all my life – pale and lifeless in a pool of his own blood. It made me grateful for my loss of sight. At any moment, I could rip that blindfold off and stop seeing. I had a terrible feeling, though, that I could never unsee this. It would surface again in the dark hours or when the ghouls came to play.

Away across town at the south end of the village, there was a little cottage with a woman and three children who would never hear Woodreaver's voice again. I knew them all. I'd be watching them grasp to try to understand this night for months and years to come.

My throat felt fuzzy at the thought. Something was roaring in my ears.

I cleared my throat.

"We were just walking," Fletcher said, stuttering. He was twice my age. Maybe more. Closer to forty than thirty. So was Woodreaver.

I watched him with narrowing eyes. What had they been doing out in the woods in the middle of the night? That was no time for woodcutting or gathering feathers to make arrows.

I crossed my arms over my chest.

"At night. In the woods."

His eyes grew sharp and flicked to mine. "It's not what you think."

But I was only seventeen and the protected daughter of the Hunter. I could tell he meant something significant, but I couldn't tell what it was. What shameful thing did he think I suspected him of? I made my face cold and hard. I'd pretend I knew until I found out.

"What was it then?"

He looked nervous. A small part of me found that interesting. After all, I was the one barely out of childhood. Shouldn't he be wondering what *I* was doing out? But it didn't work that way. Guilt was a powerful thing and it didn't stop to think about what other people might be up to when it was busy clobbering you into the ground.

I understood that.

"Just something ..." his voice trailed off and my eyes widened under my blindfold at the smell on his breath.

"You've been drinking." And that reminded me of my father grumbling one winter a few years ago to my mother. There had been a fire in the woods. In the winter. A strange thing – unheard-of even. He'd said something about "fools and their drink" and my mother had whispered about a hidden 'still.' I didn't know what that was, and they hadn't been interested in telling me. "You have a still in the woods."

It was a gamble, but I saw it struck a nerve when he nodded.

"These woods are full of faerie creatures now," I said grimly. "From now on, things like stills are luxuries you can't have. Help me with Woodreaver. He's too heavy for me alone."

Fletcher nodded and his movements were the quick movements of relief as we worked to lift Fletcher.

We carried him to the village. I was barely able to do my part. If it had just been me and not Fletcher, too, I wouldn't have made it.

I was huffing and exhausted as we passed the first windows glowing with light. I concentrated on my feet, each step an effort almost to the peak of my capacity.

Too heavy. He was too heavy. My arms and chest ached from the effort.

The road running north to south was bright in the moonlight and I fought my aching limbs as I tried to match Fletcher's stride. We passed the smithy and the inn – lit up despite the lateness of the hour – and reached the square.

I'd been so focused on my burden that I hadn't noticed the crowd gathering. The murmurs were unsettling.

"… creepy with that blindfold on but walking like she can see …"

And then in horror, "Oh sweet stars, it's Woodreaver!"

"Someone go get his Goodie!"

"Go for Goodie Herben, too. Quickly, now!"

"… gored right through!"

It wasn't until we set him down that I looked up and saw that almost everyone was gathered – most of the adults in the town. They showed signs of hasty dress – nightshirts tucked into breeches. Shawls thrown around nightdresses despite the warmth of an early Autumn evening.

Their faces were grim as they looked at Woodreaver's husk lying dead in the square. His face had lost the look of humanity, changing to something unfamiliar.

Fletcher sat down on the street beside his friend and began to sob. I felt the tight grip of nervousness seize my heart. I didn't know if it was grief or drink that had rendered him so useless to me, but these people were already upset with me. Already certain I was to blame for losing Chanter and Hunter. What would they do now that I'd brought Woodreaver to their door? Especially when my only witness was a drunken mess?

"What happened here," a frosty voice asked. It was Alebren – the innkeeper. He crossed his arms over his chest.

"Careful now, Little Hunter," Scouvrel whispered. "This has the look of a mob. I quite like mobs. They are delightfully blind and the games you can play with them can be tempting – but are you ready to play?"

"I found him in the woods. Dead," I said, ignoring Scouvrel. The truth was my only weapon here.

Alebren looked around the ring of townspeople and a look entered his face that I didn't understand. But as Goodie Thatcher smiled at him from across the circle, it couldn't be good. I searched the ring for my mother, but I didn't see her there. I didn't see Goodie Chanter either. My mouth went dry.

"This is what we talked about when you chose me as mayor just a few hours ago."

Mayor? Our tiny village had never had a mayor.

"There's nothing like conflict to bring out the power-hungry. How delightful." Scouvrel's words sent chills through me. I grabbed his cage – still tied to my belt with my free hand, swallowing against the rush of nerves that filled me.

"Did you kill the creature that killed him, Alastra Hunter?" the new mayor asked.

"No," I said. "I'm going back out – "

He raised a hand, interrupting me. "You will not raise a hand against the faerie creatures. No one will until the Knights of Light arrive."

"But it killed Woodreaver," I protested. "It has my arrow stuck in its haunch."

The mayor *tsked*. "You Hunters only look for violence everywhere. Look at what you've done to our peaceful town."

He pointed at Woodreaver's corpse. There was a rustle of movement on the edge of the crowd and then Goodie Woodreaver's wail tore through the night as she pushed through the ring of people and threw herself across the breast of her dead husband.

My head swam and my throat burned with nausea.

"Look at the tragedy your family has brought," the mayor said sternly. "Hunter is an old occupation. Old as the storms of winter – and just as unnecessary. We've met and decided together that there is to be no more village hunter. It's not an occupation we need. We will not provoke them. We will wait until the Knights come and determine how to handle this crisis. Perhaps, a great lord or lady will take pity on Skundton and take us under their wing."

I felt my mouth drop open. I shut it with a snap.

"And what about the unicorn that did that?" I asked in horror, pointing to Woodreaver.

"You said yourself that you put your arrow into it," the mayor said quietly.

"But –"

He held up a hand. "Did she shoot before or after he was gored, Fletcher?"

Fletcher seemed to shake himself, his drunken sobs fading for a moment. "I don't know."

"Think," Mayor Alebren asked and for the first time in my life, I saw an avaricious glitter behind his usually docile eyes.

"I ... it could have been before," Fletcher said. Traitor.

"It wasn't," I protested. "Unless someone stops it, it will gore more people. It will take the Knights weeks to arrive. Weeks where you will all fall prey to faerie creatures unless I stop them!"

"Enough, Allie," the new mayor said. "We won't bother the faerie creatures and they won't bother us."

But it didn't work like that. Predators hunted. It was what they did. Humans only survived if we hunted better. I opened my mouth to speak but he spoke loudly, so the whole town could hear.

"You will remove the snares you Hunters have set," he said loudly. "And you will stop hunting the lands. Until a decision is made by the Knights of Light all trapping and hunting will cease. This is our decision for Skundton."

"And if I refuse?" I asked and a hush fell over the gathered townsfolk. They hadn't expected that from me. Maybe if I had been Hulanna – bold and beautiful, but not Alastra with her acidic comments and taciturn nature.

The mayor sighed. "You put us all at risk. We've suffered enough."

He gestured to where Goodie Woodreaver was still huddled over her husband, her sobs shaking them both, and I felt a painful tug at my heart. I didn't even like the Woodreavers much, and their pain nearly crippled me. And it would hurt just as much if it was anyone in this town. This place was all I knew, and I knew it well – knew every person, every animal, every path and nook and hiding place.

I should know where the key was to open the portal. I should have already solved that riddle and freed my father and sister. If I had, none of this would have happened.

"Your mother is staying with the Thatchers," Mayor Alebren said and I gasped. My mother would not have chosen to stay with the Thatchers. Of that, I was sure. There was steel in his voice as he continued. "Bring your snares and any other weapons you possess to the inn tomorrow and the two of you can go back to your cottage and raise your goats. But no more killing. No more death."

I felt the rough hands at my back and tried to spin but someone had dragged my quiver from me before I could stop them – their sudden attack so surprising to me, who had never feared harm from my own town – that I didn't think to anticipate it.

"That's my bow and arrows," I said through numb lips as if even they could hardly stand to admit this betrayal.

"You won't need them now," the Mayor said with a tone of superiority. "We are a peaceful town. And I'll hang the next person to break the peace."

My gasp wasn't the only one filling the square as he turned and called to a man at the back of the crowd. "Gravedigger!"

Gravedigger shuffled forward with Goodie Gravedigger at his side. She shot me a pitying look that gutted me. Because I realized in that moment that even if anyone disagreed with the new mayor, no one was going to say so. No one was going to give me back my bow or the title of Hunter. It was all I was. And it was gone now, too.

I watched numbly as they took Woodreaver away and as the new mayor strode back to the inn. Watched numbly as the good people of Skundton returned to their homes.

My heart felt deadly cold.

And then, as if the very world felt my same icy pain, snow began to fall softly over our town. Snow in the heat of harvest.

I didn't even have enough warmth left in me to feel surprised.

Chapter Thirty-Six

"I can see why this town is so popular," Scouvrel said snidely as I sat down on the rim of the well in the center of the town. "The people here have all the charms of the Lord of Cups."

"Then I hope I never meet him," I growled.

I pulled my blindfold off and looked at him for the first time since our deal. Was he looking even prettier than usual? His dark hair framed his face perfectly and his smoky wings only highlighted his bare chest and back, the feather tattoos running up his arms seemed to make his hands disappear into the night, except for where one held an embroidery needle like a sword. His jacket had been cleaned and was hanging from a thread tied to one of the bars – drying, I thought.

"Are you cold?" I asked – more for something to say than for real concern. He'd spread the cloth out under him, and the edges of it reached up along the bottom of the bars so that if I moved and he slid across the floor of the cage he should hit cloth and not iron.

"No," he said with a glittering smile. "But some people say my heart is made of ice."

"I'll take that under advisement," I said, but my mind was elsewhere. I had a decision to make. Would I give the town my father's other bows and arrows and our snares to gain my mother's freedom, or would I try again to go through the Star Stone circle and get him back?

I could imagine life without him or Hulanna – just my mother and me in the cottage with the goats. We could live like that. But I knew it would hollow her. It would hollow me. And eventually, the grinding hate already sprouting in my heart would eat me up until one black night when I –

"Did you know we can hear wicked thoughts sometimes? Yours are black indeed," Scouvrel said.

"What's it to you?"

He shrugged. "As long as I'm your captive I'd prefer that you didn't kill yourself. Who knows what will befall me then?"

I grunted.

When I gamed it out in my mind, going through the circle was the only solution I could stomach. My mother would understand. And she would find a way to free herself. He was better with people than I was.

But I would need the key. I wondered if that poem I'd read in the book could actually help me find it? I said it aloud, trying to remember every word.

"In a ring but deep you go," I muttered.

Scouvrel snickered.

"In a spot the wind can't blow."

His smile turned wicked and he looked at me as if he would like to make me wicked, too.

"Buried deep but not in dirt."

He licked his lips.

"Hold your breath. With death, you flirt."

"Adorable," he said, stretching out the word as if he was tasting it for the first time. "You're a poet. Do you always speak verse about the things you sit on? You could sit on me. I could use another poem inspired by my great prowess."

"*Another* poem?" I asked dryly. "Yeah, that checks out."

But my mind was on his words and the glitter in his eye.

A poem about what I was sitting on.

The well.

It was older than the town – the first thing to be built here.

I thought through the lines of the poem. He was right. That could mean a well. And the key could be buried under the water. I'd have to hold my breath to get it. And it must be a long way under if I was going to flirt with death to get it.

"It's going to be dark under there," I muttered.

"How about a game," Scouvrel said.

"Do I look like I'm in the mood to play games?" I hissed, scanning the town square. One by one the town lights had snuffed out until it was only the inn still lit. The shafts of orange light sliced across the square, but they wouldn't be visible from inside the well. I shivered at the thought of dipping under the water in the middle of this driving snow.

"I'm always in the mood for a good game," Scouvrel said. "And this one will help you."

"How?" I put as much venom as I could into that one word.

"Well, it won't be nice to go underwater. A game might take your mind off of it. Besides, if you find what you are look-ing for, you'll need me to use it. Why not play my game and if you win, I will teach you how to use the key."

"And if you win?"

"I'll take another kiss."

"Who thought you'd be so desperate for a scrap of affec-tion," I muttered, but it worried me that his eyes lit dangerously at that – as if I had struck a nerve.

"What kind of game?" I asked, untying the cage from my belt. He watched me speculatively as I set his cage down in the gathering snow.

"Truth or lie," he said, smiling.

"I thought you could only tell the truth."

If I went into the well, I couldn't go in fully clothed. My clothes would drag at me, and if they were wet when I came back to the surface, I might die of hypothermia. Reluctantly, I began to disrobe, folding my wool cloak first so that the inside would stay snow-free and then shucking off my boots and belt.

"Or we could play *Seduction*," Scouvrel said speculatively as I undressed. "I love that game."

I glanced around me, hoping no one was peering out of their window. "Shut up."

"Truth or lie it is," he said with a wide grin.

I tried not to look at him as I stripped down the rest of the way but slipped my blindfold back on for one last task. Awkwardly, I dropped the bucket into the well, letting all the rope spool out and then double-checking the knot on the end. Would it hold my weight? It would have to.

"Truth or lie – you look lovely naked in the snow," he said.

"I'm not naked. I kept my smallclothes on."

He laughed.

I pulled the blindfold off and left it on my heap of clothes and shot him a look that should kill. "Why don't you stick to less personal topics?"

This time his laughter was full-throated. He was enjoying this.

"Then you'll play?"

"Why not," I muttered. "But the specifics of the reward will be determined at the end."

"I promise," he said, holding up a hand, "that you can add all the qualifiers needed to put me back in the cage as long as you give me the kiss."

I rolled my eyes at him and jammed the handle of the cage in my mouth. I didn't dare leave it up here while I was down the well. What if someone stole it? What if they opened the door?

I felt blindly for my belt and then looped my belt through the handle and fastened it. I could tie it to the rope on the way down.

It was hard to feel my way out to the waiting rope. I was too afraid to lose my balance by reaching out too far and too blind to actually see the rope.

"A little to your right," Souvrel said helpfully.

I said nothing. My mouth was full.

Catching the rope, I added the grip of my other hand and before I could chicken out, I threw my weight onto it, dangling in the darkness over a certain drop.

Here we go.

This had better work.

Chapter Thirty-Seven

My hands were already numb from the cold as I slid down the rough well rope. I was taking my time. I didn't want to open the flesh of my palms by actually sliding, so I was using the method my father had taught me long ago, using hands and feet, the rope twisted a specific way around my left calf as a safety measure.

Careful, Allie. Deep breaths. Careful movements. My bare flesh was pebbled from the cold already. Blind in the dark, the only way I would know that I'd reached the water would be when my feet touched it and then things would only get colder.

I wished there was a spirit trail here, and it worried me that there wasn't. Maybe it was just because the well had been used so much that it dissipated while the cave the cage had been in was only used intermittently. Or maybe I was on a wild goose chase. I'd chased wild geese on the high plains with my father, kicking up lingering ghouls as I ran laughing at the huge flocks. Father liked goose jerky. Everyone did. We usually sold it for Winter Night.

I tried not to think of Winter Night as my teeth chattered.

"Truth or Lie," Scouvrel said from his cage. "I have danced on these lands in my dreams and I saw you there."

"It's a pathetic game," I said through chattering teeth. "Because you can't lie."

"Or maybe that's the lie – that we can't lie. Maybe it's only something humans say about us."

"Truth," I said, gritting my teeth. The rope seemed longer than I remembered. Did all these Fae say 'oh I dreamed about you' and expect girls to turn like butter in their palms? If I was butter, then I was winter butter – cold and hard. "It's the truth."

"Yes. Your turn."

"Truth or Lie," I said. "I meant to kill you when I put you in the cage."

"Truth," he said. "Try asking something harder."

"You knew that, and you weren't scared?"

"Truth or Lie?" he asked, ignoring the question. "You liked being kissed by me."

His eyes were a little too bright as he asked that. Like he was dying to know the answer. Well, int hat case, he wouldn't get one.

"Whatever I answer, you'll say it's wrong," I said. "You're cheating."

I flinched, hissing through my teeth as my toes touched the cold water. With care, trying no to lose the grip of my feet on the rope, I tied the belt to it.

"I'm not cheating. I'm gleaning information. What better way to play a game?" Scouvrel winked at me and I scowled in the darkness. At least I could see him.

"Hopefully, the knot holds, and you don't drown before I get back," I said.

"I'm charmed by your concern."

"Don't be."

I dropped from the rope before he could reply, sucking in a breath as I fell and wincing as I plunged into the water. The moment I passed the surface, I could see a golden trail through the water. I turned in the close confines of the stone well and kicked hard, chasing after it. At least I knew something was here. I wasn't chasing shadows. The rough rope brushed my leg – my only connection back to the land of air and sky.

How far down would I have to go? I could envision the slimy walls of the well around me, the rough stones slick from centuries of use. I'd seen it in low water years, when the surface of the water seemed a thousand leagues away. None of us knew how deep it went – only that we'd never failed to find water here no matter how bad the drought.

Would I have enough breath to make it to the key – to make it back after I got it? How deep would my ancestors have hidden it?

I tried not to panic. That would only make it worse.

It felt exactly like the poem – like I was flirting with death going down here. Like I was in the very throat of the grave. If my mother knew what I was doing, she might faint with fear.

My mother. My father. Hulanna. I must succeed for them.

I tried to make my fear burn to fuel me. To propel me downward into the inky depths.

Perhaps Hulanna wasn't really my enemy at all. Perhaps it had only appeared that way when she arrived in the circle. Perhaps all of that was nothing more than glamor.

I kicked harder. My lungs were beginning to burn, and still, the golden trail went deeper.

I wasn't going to make it. I didn't have enough breath.

And now I could think of nothing except for how much my lungs hurt – hurt so very much.

They were screaming when the golden trail finally ended in a tiny nook in the side of the well. I jammed my hand into the darkness – a missing stone if I had to guess – and found the key wedged inside. Frustrated, I yanked at it, pulling.

I was running out of time.

I was going to die like this.

Fury filled me at the unfairness of it all. That I – Alastra Hunter – would die in a stupid well with a leering Faerie while I tried to take a key that no one should have hidden here in the first place!

The key shifted.

I twisted my hand and it came free.

Not enough time!

I kicked up toward the surface, pain blinding every part of me as I fought, desperately for the surface. I wasn't going to make it.

I could feel my consciousness fading.

Let it fuel you, Allie!

I needed to breathe.

Panic filled me and I kicked harder, lashing out so that the rocks bruised and battered my hands and feet.

I pulled in a lungful of water, choking, drowning, dying.

And then my head broke the surface and I was coughing, spewing out water, puking out every last ounce of it as I clung to the rope. I didn't think I could hold on. I was going to lose my grip. I was going to drown.

"And you said I should groom. You're swimming in your own vomit."

Fury at him for mocking me in my weakness bubbled to the surface and I wrapped my trembling leg around the rope and pushed up to where the cage was.

"Although, shockingly, I would still love to kiss you," the Fae teased.

"You're the worst," I wheezed, taking the belt from the rope and fastening it around my waist. I couldn't carry it in my teeth right now – could barely breathe even through my mouth. I leaned my head against the rope, clinging but too weak to climb.

If I didn't start climbing, I would weaken more and then I would die down here of hypothermia or drowning.

And I'd pollute the town's well even worse than I already had.

"Says the girl who just strapped me to her mostly un-clothed body," Scouvrel said, reminding me of how my thin un-derthings clung to my wet skin.

He shouldn't be looking! It was humiliating! Anger gave me the strength I needed to climb. Climbing harder as he kept talking.

"I know it's impossible to find human men as lovely as me in your world, but if you have to resort to trapping your lovers and tying them to your mostly naked body, then you're doing something wrong."

"I hate you," I gasped. My throat was raw and agonized and it still felt like I had water in my lungs. I felt like I might drown in it. But my fury at his words drove me upward until I reached the wood beam the rope hung from and with one last burst of rage, swung the rope to the rock ledge and fell over the side of it into the thin layer of snow.

The cage clanged against the rock and Scouvrel swore loudly.

"Serves you right," I moaned into the snow. "For the things you said."

"You should be thanking me," he hissed. "I just saved your life."

Chapter Thirty-Eight

When I was fourteen, I had thought that Olen might dance with me at the Skylights Festival. The whole town was excited because Queen Anabetha had been crowned in the city of Faramore and had sent nightbursts to every village she laid claim to in celebration of her coronation. Apparently, Skundton was within her borders, and our nightburst had been brought by peddler the day before.

"You won't see a ghoul in the forest for months after we set this off," he'd promised us.

I'd shyly hinted to Olen that I would certainly like to dance this year and he'd smiled that secret smile of his that suggested he would make that wish come true.

But that night, as I'd lingered at the edge of the dance, hoping for my chance, Heldra had sauntered over.

"I've decided to dance with Olen all night," she declared, smiling at Hulanna. "Isn't that sweet of me when so many other girls would hold that limp against him?"

I glanced to where Olen had been standing for the last ten minutes, looking nervously at his hands. He looked up at me, his face flushed, and then he looked at Heldra and his gaze stuck with her for the rest of the night. I should have known then that there was more there than just Heldra's usual bullying.

"It's a pity that there aren't any boys as nice as me, don't you think, Allie?" Heldra asked. "Then one of them might decide to dance with a plain girl all night and you wouldn't have to stand here looking so wilted."

Rage had filled me, but it was Hulanna who spoke, leaning in with her usual sweet half-dreamy expression as she said, "I heard Branchtrimmer's son is marrying Lacey Turnhill."

Heldra's face blanched and she stalked away. Everyone knew she'd been walking out with Daelen Branchtrimmer until last month when he'd started walking out with Lacey.

"That wasn't very nice," I had said slowly.

"No one treats my sister like that," Hulanna had said quietly and then looked at me. "Don't dance with Olen. He has two left feet."

I would have danced with him if he had no feet at all and just wooden nubs like old Minebasher did. But I didn't have the chance that night nor any night after.

Chapter Thirty-Nine

It was all I could do to get us back to the tent up on the mountain plain and start a fire. It took five times longer than it should have. My fingers were thick and clumsy, my mind clouded, and every part of me exhausted. If it hadn't been for Scouvrel's taunting and needling, I would have given up and passed out somewhere. I might even have died of cold. I just couldn't seem to make myself care.

I thought I might be hallucinating when something the Scouvrel called an owlgriffin swooped past, turned to land on the other side of the fire, and cuddled down in the long grass and snow as I finally got the wood to light. I didn't even remember taking a blanket from the tent or using it to cover Scouvrel's cage and my exhausted body.

When I woke it was long past dawn. Someone was calling my name.

"Allie? Are you there?" I gasped. Olen!

I was up on my feet before I realized anything else, pushing my tangled hair – frozen with bits of grass stuck to it where it had laid on the frosty ground – out of my eyes and trying as fast as possible to comb the ice out with my fingers and braid it back into my usual over-the-shoulder braid.

"Could you at least take the blanket off the cage?" Scouvrel complained.

I shoved the blindfold up and carefully took the blanket from his cage.

"Allie?" Olen called.

"I'm here!" my voice was harsh and raspy. I coughed, my lungs aching at the effort. I'd breathed in water last night. I should have died.

I wanted to sob at the memory, but girls who just found a *second* artifact to save their people didn't cry. I stiffened my spine instead and burned off that ... whatever that emotion was ... feeding into my fire within.

Olen was in front of me before I was tidy again. I scrubbed at my eyes and face, dislodging frozen grass and pine needles. I probably looked like a mess. I felt like a tangle of hopes and hurts.

He was taking his time, each step painful by the way he winced.

"Let me boil the kettle," I said thickly, but he shook his head. He didn't sit. He just stared at me and I felt my face coloring.

"So, you're out," he said.

I looked around at the open plain. I certainly hadn't slept under a roof. "It would appear so."

"I mean you aren't Hunter anymore. You're out of a job."

I thought Scouvrel made me angry last night, but it was nothing compared to the fury I felt at his cold words. He didn't care. I saw the mandolin hanging from the strap on his back.

"Are you here to play?" I asked, ice coating every word.

He didn't care that my world had been snatched away.

"No one cares about this stupid circle anymore, Allie," He said with a shake of his head.

So why had he walked all the way up here when it hurt him to cross the cottage?

"I thought you cared. You were the one that was so intent on guarding it." I threw the challenge into my words.

Help me! I thought at him. Help me guard it! Help me save them!

He kicked at the frozen grass. "I was a fool. The mayor is right. The only threat here came because we were here stirring things up. We made it worse. If we leave it alone, then the threat is gone."

"What about your father?" I put a hand on one of my hips.

"He's gone, too." His tone was harsh – haunted.

I snorted, shaking my head. "Then what are you doing here?"

"I heard what the town said to you. I'm here to help you take down your snares and turn in your bows. I care about you, Allie. I don't want to see you get in trouble."

My head felt fuzzy, like maybe the rage had burned up rational thought. He was here to dismantle me? To take me apart a bit at a time – and he thought he was doing me a *favor*?

"I thought it was Heldra you cared about." I made my words steel.

He looked away, his cheeks staining red. "I care about you, too."

At my loud scoff, his eyes shot back to me and he took a wobbling step, threw an arm around my waist, and kissed me. It was so unexpected that it took me a moment to even react.

I'd always liked Olen. I'd thought about kissing him. I'd thought about a lot of things.

And yet.

Not like this. Not when he didn't trust me.

I didn't like it. It felt like he was only doing it to get something out of me.

Worse, I couldn't help but compare it to the kiss I'd shared with Scouvrel yesterday. He'd *wanted* to kiss me. It had been the reward, not the tool to get a reward. That kiss had been ... well, I was still thinking about it even now, still tingling and blushing at the thought of it. Not like this one. This one felt dull and lifeless. I should want it after dreaming about it for years, and yet it was hollow.

He finished and pulled back, his eyes blazing with more than passion – with irritation.

"What was that for?" I challenged.

"You can come back, Allie. Come back to life in Skundton and it can be like it always was. We'll be friends. We'll sit on the sidelines and watch people and talk. We'll eat ourselves sick on goat cheese curds and honey at dances and help our mothers bring in the firewood and we'll put all of this – trauma – behind us. Come back with me."

"And what?" I asked and my voice was harsher than I meant it to be because that didn't sound like a happy future to me. It didn't have my father or Hulanna in it. And it didn't have me as the town Hunter in it. And it didn't account for what might happen if the circle opened again. It was a future for people with their heads shoved in a snowbank. A future for idiots. A cold wind erupted, blowing icy particles across our faces and making me hide in my cloak. "What comes after that? Are you going to marry Heldra still?"

He looked away.

"Then why did you kiss me?" I couldn't keep the bite from my words. The kiss was bitter on my lips.

He sounded pained when he said, "Come on, Allie."

"Did your mother send you?"

He bit his lip and then shook his head irritably. "Your mom isn't happy with the Thatchers. But she can come live with us if you just give in and stop all this pig-headedness. My mom – well, she wants her friend back."

"Your *mom* sent you to kiss me?" My voice rose to a pitch that I'd never heard before. He had the grace to look even more embarrassed. "What about your father? Doesn't she want him back?"

The breath hissed out of him. "Of course, she does!"

"Well, giving up isn't the way to do that, Olen! We have to fight! We have to find a way to get back into that circle and get him back!"

"Would you just leave off, Allie?" he shouted, his expression twisting with anger.

My own anger swelled to join it, pushing at my self-control with the same strength as the wind howling around us.

"You're an idiot, Olen Chanter. And a coward. Why can't you just *try* for once?"

He leaned in close, his words like daggers. "Why can't you just be a normal girl for once instead of an angry freak."

"What are you talking about?" And something cold and painful whipsawed through my anger. Something that whispered that I did know what he was talking about even if I pretended that I didn't. That I'd always known that was how people saw me. That it was true.

"You've always got to have a problem to solve, Allie. You're always angry about something you think you can fix. You never trust anyone. You can't be happy. And now you want to make all of us miserable with you."

"You shouldn't have come here." I enunciated every word so there would be no mistake. And I forced the tremble from my lips and let the fury fill me instead. But I couldn't help the way my whole body was shaking. Rage would do that to a person.

Did they think I'd be a good girl and just give up? Then they didn't know me.

I didn't give up on anything.

And I wasn't a good girl.

"You're right," Olen said stiffly. "It was a waste of my time."

He was storming away, before I could say anything more, the wind whipping his cloak almost off his retreating figure. I let myself break into tears. It was fine to cry now, when no one could see me. Fine to feel awful when no one could learn my weakness.

My tears soaked my blindfold as I slid into the tent, set the cage beside the small bedroll, and sat down on it with a thump. Outside, the icy wind tore at the tent. Inside, I was frozen more than just physically. I felt like ice crawled through my veins as something solidified inside me.

Tomorrow, I was going to catch that unicorn. And then I was going to use the key and go through the circle and free my father and sister. And no one was going to stop me. Not Olen. Not the whole town.

"Truth or Lie," Scouvrel asked from the darkness. "You're in love with that human boy."

"Lie," I hissed. But my answer was the real lie.

Chapter Forty

I didn't cry as I packed up my camp and put it in the pack my mother had given me. To give in to that would be to admit that the rejection of the town and everyone except my family had left wounds in me that I could feel – and I would never give them that satisfaction. Especially Olen.

When I was finished packing up, I lit a fire again. I set the cage beside the fire once it was lit. Only then did I take off my blindfold and examine the key.

"Truth or lie," Scouvrel said. "It's the loveliest thing you've ever seen."

"Lie," I said. The loveliest thing I'd ever seen was him, but I'd never admit to that.

"Truth or lie," I asked, trying not to flush at my thoughts. "You know how to use this key."

"I know how to open the circle," he agreed.

"With the key?" I specified. It was gorgeous – golden in appearance, though likely not made from real gold. No one in Skundton had gold. Certainly not this much of it.

"I can open it at any time," he said.

"And can you tell me how to open it?" I asked.

I tried willing the key to open the circle. Nothing happened.

"Our game still isn't complete," Scouvrel said. "I don't interrupt games. Not for anything. Didn't you read the rules in that book of yours?"

I snorted, getting up and examining each stone for a keyhole. I checked the grass, looking for a lock of any kind, but when an hour had passed and I'd examined every inch of the area with both regular sight and spiritual sight, I had to give up. There was no way to use the key.

"Truth or Lie?" Scouvrel asked. "You need to capture the unicorn to use the key."

I shot him an eagle-eyed look. "Truth?"

He grinned.

Great. For that, I needed a weapon. And the town had taken my bow.

I turned the key over in my hands again.

"What's the point of making a key that doesn't do anything? That doesn't work?" I complained.

"It works," Scouvrel said. "You're just doing it wrong."

"Truth or lie?" I asked grumpily as I packed up my flint and knife. "You are cold without your shirt on in this icy wind."

"Lie." His tone was playful. "Only my heart is cold."

Then he would be fine. I tried not to look at the way his skin pebbled against the wind or the way his muscles flexed as he braced against it. It wasn't fair to look. I hadn't liked it when he'd looked at so much of *my* skin last night.

He untied his jacket from the bar, shaking it out to try to unthaw it enough to put on his body. It was stiff with frost and cold. The muscles of his shoulders and arms flexed as he worked.

With a grunt of frustration, I pulled my blindfold back on and started out to my family's cottage.

The forest trails were too quiet. I kept my blindfold on and watched them with worry. Not a chipmunk chittered, or a squirrel scolded. Not a raven cawed or a chickadee called. Not a rabbit broke out in front of us or a partridge flew up at our passing. None of the shadows contained a single ghoul.

Yes, it was windy and cold. Yes, the storm clouds were building over Skundton suggesting more bad weather to come. And yet, I didn't think that should mean that it would be so quiet here.

I found the buck just outside the area we kept clear for our cottage. He lay dead right on the trail, his magnificent rack so wide that my father probably would have hung it over the shed door if he was here. But there was no arrow in the buck. Instead, massive gore marks plunged into his chest. Three of them – as wide as my fist. I hissed at the sight. The unicorn.

I couldn't see his tracks, though, and it wasn't until I pulled down my blindfold that I could see signs of his passing by – a purple glowing trail winding through the woods.

I grunted.

"Truth or Lie," Scouvrel asked. "I trapped a unicorn when I was a child and it granted me a wish."

"Sounds like a lie to me," I said. "Nothing in this world grants wishes."

He snickered. "Now isn't that a nasty cold heart you have, Little Hunter. And just so you know, I'm winning the game right now."

"Truth or Lie? You cheat."

"Always."

I didn't like to admit it, but the sight of the buck had shaken me. I knew how powerful a strong buck like that could be – how precise an arrow would have to be to take him down – how even a shot right to the eye might not do it. They could run and run and run even when they were dying. This one hadn't run at all. Its blood pooled in the grass and snow, smelling heavily of the autumn rut.

I cleared my throat and made toward our home, pulling the blindfold back into place.

I broke through the trees beside the goat pen and gasped.

Something had slaughtered our goats. Something inhuman. Trails of guts, pools of blood and scraps of fur were scattered over the fences like horrific streamers for a party I hadn't been invited to. There was no part of a goat more than a few inches long that was left in one piece. But there were plenty of scraps. Enough for me to know that all of our herd was dead and most of it hadn't even been eaten.

I felt my gorge rise in my throat. Feral faerie creatures. This was their work.

"Truth or Lie?" I asked hoarsely. "Your kind kills for fun."

"Truth," Scouvrel whispered.

The door of my cottage hung open and my footsteps slowed to a shuffle as I watched it sway in the wind. We didn't leave our door open. Especially not in the cold. Someone – or something – might be in there. I drew my hunting knife in one hand, too chilled and too afraid to move quickly. Step by step, I inched into the house, looking in every direction.

My mother's cottage was always neat as a pin. Nothing out of place. Smelling of herbs and vinegar and cleanliness. I'd never seen it like this before.

Everything we owned was broken and strewn across the floors. The stuffing had been pulled out of the mattresses. The blankets had been ripped. The food dumped out over the floor. I shuffled through the mess, wary and searching, checking with care behind every door and in each rafter. I saved the attic for last. It was empty. It hadn't even been trashed like the rest.

But there wasn't a weapon in the house. Every arrow, every bow – even the ones that needed repair – were gone.

"Truth or Lie?" Scouvrel asked me gently. "Humans did this."

"Truth," I whispered. And wrath bubbled up inside me.

It was a good thing that they'd asked me not to be their Hunter anymore. Because the thing I saw that was harming our village right now – the predator that was out of control – was humans. And I wanted to hunt them almost as badly as I wanted to hunt Fae.

I hurried out to the shed. The search party must have either forgotten to search it or had found the jumble of half-broken items and messy unspooled rope enough of a mess that they hadn't felt the need to add to it. What they didn't realize was that this was my father's world, while the house was my mother's world. For every clean corner of the cottage, there was a messy corner here. For every folded blanket she had, he had a tangled rope. For every neat string of drying herbs she kept, he had an old barrel of arrows and assorted long items in need of repair. For every nice weapon he kept in her world, he had a dozen less-than-perfect ones strewn under tangled piles of junk in here.

I found one of his old bows – left over from his boyhood and treasured by him but far too small for a man's draw now – under a tangle of assorted ropes and dried leaves. It would be perfect for me. Found a bow with a broken shaft under a tangle of half-whittled staves. From it, I pulled a perfectly useful well-oiled string and restrung my father's boyhood bow.

It took longer to find useful arrows. But my father hung on to arrows and he had a tendency to lose things in plain sight. It would be a mistake to think that everything in this shed was past repair. It was a mistake I didn't make.

I found six good arrows and an old slightly-moldy quiver that was still more than suitable for use. I dragged a mouse nest made of deer hair out from the bottom of the quiver and filled it with my arrows.

Ha! I'd show those villagers. And they'd all regret the ultimatum they gave me. They'd regret trashing our home. They'd regret taking my mom captive.

I was going to hunt down that unicorn, use the key, and set my father free and then they'd all pay.

I didn't realize I was laughing darkly under my breath until Scouvrel joined me. I stopped abruptly. Anything he found funny was probably wicked.

"Truth or Lie?" I asked. "You're the most wicked thing I've ever met."

He laughed harder. "Wouldn't you like to know."

Chapter Forty-One

Tracking the unicorn was easy as long as my blindfold was off. Or at least, it was easy to see where it went. It was hard not to hit trees as I stalked through the woods.

"Oof!" I said for what felt like the thousandth time as a leaning willow's branches smacked me in the face. If I wasn't so furious about everything that had happened, I might have felt sorry for myself, but I had no room for any other feelings. The rage inside me grew with every hour that I stalked through the woods, warming me, singing to me, filling me up.

"Truth or Lie?" Scouvrel whispered. "Revenge is sweet."

I didn't answer. I was sick of his game. And who knew if it would be sweet? I didn't want revenge. I just wanted to prove that I was right and that they were idiots. I wanted Olen to see that I wasn't a freak. I wanted my mom to be proud of me. I wanted them all to beg me to be Hunter again.

The unicorn moved quickly for such a large creature and by the time the sun was at the apex of the sky, it had led me back up to the mountain plains. I slid out from between the trees, looking out over the waving grass. It had snowed all morning, drifting badly in the driving wind so that piles of snow crept up along the trunks of trees on just one side, plastering it with snow all the way up while the other side was bare.

Whatever was making nature so angry suited my mood just fine. But it wasn't helping me see across the plains to where the unicorn might be. I pulled my blindfold off and then on a few times as I scanned the plains. Even with it off, I could only see the trail but not the unicorn. It seemed to lead to the center of the Sky Stone circle.

My instincts screamed at me to be careful, but I ignored them. This was what I'd come for.

I pulled the bow and an arrow out of the quiver, nocking the arrow carefully. With a deep breath, I began to stalk across the plain, blindfold down.

I could see the glowing stones around the circle – a faint white ring. I could see the bright purple path of the unicorn leading into them.

I could see nothing else. No trails away from the circle. No sign of the unicorn.

My skin crawled, tension frizzling on the end of every nerve.

Was it hiding behind the stones?

"How are you going to help me use this key, unicorn?" I muttered.

"It's the hair," Scouvrel said and I jumped.

"I know," I said, rallying. "You need to wash it."

I peered at him lounging in the center of the cage looking gorgeous as his longish hair hung over his eye despite his attempt to pull it back into a knot. His smoky wings wrapped around him like a sultry cloak.

"No," he drawled, adjusting his pose as if he could seduce me just by changing his position. "I meant the unicorn hair. It has something to do with the riddle you're trying to solve."

I snorted, tightened the cage back to my belt and got my bow ready again before stalking toward the Star Stone circle.

I eased my weight onto my toes, carefully striding through the snow as I kept my eyes on the circle. The storm was becoming a blizzard. There was no way I was going to be able to sleep up here tonight – or at home. I was going through the circle one way or another.

I gritted my teeth and plunged on through the snow.

A purple glow flickered from behind the large stones. I tried to move slowly and smoothly – as I'd seen my father do it. Tried to keep my mind focused and undistracted.

Wait.

Last time, Scouvrel had said 'boo.' In all the chaos afterward, I'd forgotten. He'd ruined my shot before. Would he ruin it this time, too? But now it was too late to change what I was doing. I would spook the unicorn and lose my chance.

My weight leaned forward on my foot so that my head ducked in through the circle of stones. The unicorn was there just as I'd hoped.

My gaze met the unicorn's. Red gleamed in the depths of his eyes as if they were showing me the fires of hell.

I was too close. I'd stepped in too close.

My heart thudded in my chest. It was hard to breathe. I couldn't run or it would gore me in the back – like it did to that buck. Like it did to Woodreaver.

I held my ground, my heart in my throat. I brought my arrow in line carefully, drawing ... drawing ... waiting, finding my perfect shot ...

Now, Allie!

I loosed the arrow.

The unicorn reared up at the same second that I fired. The arrow passed under its body uselessly. It had spun and was charging toward me before I could draw a second arrow.

No, no, no!

"Bad shot," Scouvrel hissed and I didn't know if he was teasing me or actually worried for me. It almost sounded like worry.

I tried to grab another arrow anyway, my mouth dry, fear tearing through me like the icy wind. I fumbled with it, dropping it in my haste. It was too late. I could see the almost-human gleam in the unicorn's eye as if it was just as sentient as Scouvrel – just as faerie as he was.

The unicorn reared, but I didn't dare turn my back on it, though I dodged to the side of its pawing hooves. Its breath gusted over me in the cold air, leaving streams of steam hanging like small clouds. My heart was in my throat. I couldn't breathe.

Think, Allie, think!

The cage clattered against my leg.

And just like that, it came to me.

I focused my eyes on the unicorn, my hand drifting to the cage, caressing it.

The unicorn was just a horse with a horn. Just a creature like any other. Nothing special, I told myself. A thing of bone and blood. A thing of the earth that would return to the earth someday.

I drew in a long, steadying breath as his hooves hit the ground and the snow stopped falling abruptly.

Just a thing of dirt. No more special or magical than any living thing.

I looked in its eye, defiance roaring through me. I refused to think about why it was lowering its head. Refused to look at the tip of the horn as it lowered toward me.

"No," Scouvrel whispered. "Don't do it."

I focused. Dirt. Ash. Dust. Earth.

The unicorn charged.

I closed my eyes so that nothing could distract my focus.

Nothing. He was here today, but what was today? Just a blink in the ages, a tiny spark of light in eternity. Nothing.

I felt a brush of something across my face.

When I opened my eyes, he was gone.

A hideous scream came from the cage and I untied it from my belt, raising it to eye level and almost screamed myself. Inside the cage, Scouvrel leapt to the side, barely keeping his balance as the cage swung in my grip. The unicorn – tiny now – lunged for him. His sewing needle flicked out, piercing the side of the creature and then he leapt into the air, spinning into a front flip just as the unicorn tried to impale the place where he'd been. He landed, his gorgeous muscles flexing as he stuck the landing and thrust the needle through the creature again.

Another leap and he was in the air, spinning. He landed on the back of the unicorn, gripping its mane with one hand. It bucked like mad trying to dislodge him. The cage was too small. As the unicorn bucked, he slammed Scouvrel into the iron bars and the Fae hissed in pain, red weals tracing themselves over his shoulder and back.

I gasped, horrified by what I'd done.

"Bargain with me, Hunter!" Scouvrel called through gritted teeth.

"The game," I gasped.

"Forget the game and bargain with me." His eyes were wild.

And I shouldn't have cared. I should have just been glad that all my enemies were in that cage – but I *did* care. I was starting to like that snide voice and rough snicker. If I was honest, he might be the only thing close to a friend that I had left. If I was being very honest, I'd have to admit that I didn't actually find joy in the idea of him being trampled to a pulp under the hooves of this beast, or gored to death by its sharp horn, or burned over and over again by the bars.

"Stop thinking and bargain, Hunter! Bargain with me!"

"I need to open the circle and I need to make sure that if I go in, I can save the people who went in there," I said in a rush, flinching as the unicorn reared again, smashing Scouvrel against the bars. He hissed, his smoky wings flickering.

"I will tell you how to open the circle," he said, pain searing his voice. "And I will tell you how to make it open to the one you seek. If you agree to set the unicorn free into the Faewald and out of this cage!"

The unicorn bucked again, and he nearly lost his seat, the needle flying from his grip as he held on to the glittering white mane with both hands.

"Please!" he begged, his words desperate and I felt a spike of fear shoot through me. I shouldn't make bargains without thinking, but if I didn't do it now, he would be dead, and I would lose the chance to ever learn how to open the circle again. Plus, if two of us went in, two could leave. Maybe they could be Father and Hulanna. "Please!"

"I agree!" I spat out, so nervous now that it almost seemed to overwhelm the burn of determination in my chest.

"The unicorn lost a hair when he passed you into the cage," Scouvrel said – a little breathlessly. "It's on your cloak. Take the hair, wrap it around the key and it will give you the power you need to use it to open the circle. Then step into the circle with intent, saying the name of the one you wish to see on the other side."

"That sounds like nonsense!" I objected, but I'd already found the hair.

I was already pulling my blindfold up and stashing my bow back into my quiver, retrieving my arrow, running back to gather up the pack my mother had left for me.

"What are you doing?" Scouvrel hissed. "Hurry!"

"Hold your horses," I said snidely, but it was all I could do to keep my breath normal as I slipped my blindfold off, wound the silvery unicorn hair around the key and stepped into the circle with the name on my lips.

It wasn't the name I thought I would say.

"Hulanna Hunter."

Chapter Forty-Two

When we were both sixteen, Hulanna decided she was very fond of Rootdigger's oldest son Aden. And though my parents scolded her, she often left her chores to sneak out and see him.

She found me in the goat pen one morning, watering the goats.

"I'm going to see Aden," she said, examining a dress in her hand as she held it up to the light. It was red as the apple in her other hand – a dress I'd wanted since she was given it two years before. Surprising that she'd be thinking of wearing that instead of the blue dress she favored now. "If you take the goats to pasture instead of me, I will give you what's in my hand."

I swallowed, looking at the red dress with what I knew was too much desire. She smiled as if she already knew I would say yes.

"I was headed that way anyhow," I said lightly.

But that night when I came looking for the dress, she handed me the apple.

"As agreed," she said with a smile.

She hadn't lied, I told myself. After all, it had been in her hand, too.

Chapter Forty-Three

I had expected to step into forest just like where I'd come from, only in Faewald. I should have known that this would be just as surprising as everything else had been.

I was standing in the center of a circle of stones – only unlike the stones at home, these were barely large enough to ring a campfire and they looked like skull-sized gems – polished but not cut and glowing with the warmth of rich wine.

Surrounding the stones, were massive trees – old-growth forest. They were spaced widely apart – each one large enough to hold at least four of me in a ring inside that thick trunk, their branches so high that our town could have fit under them, sheltered from storms and sun. Some of the trees – great red-leaved with gnarled bark – were large enough to hold our entire cottage inside their thick boles. They glowed with iridescent purple-red light. It was hazy twilight and small lights hung by the hundreds from the trees – or danced lightly as if they had lives of their own. Perhaps they did.

Between the trees, flickers of creatures – hundreds of them in a thousand forms – flashed in an out of existence in my spirit vision. Owl griffins sailed through the air with hawks and raven, starlings and jaybirds. None concerned that it was twilight or that they should be finding roost for the night or out beginning their hunt. Foxes slipped through the inky shadows and rabbits scrambled in the thick carpet of dead wine-colored underfoot.

Through it all snow swirled, sparkling in the lights, white against the charcoal and lavender of twilight, and so sparse as to be more decoration than winter's first claim on the land.

And everywhere I looked, there were Fae. Gorgeous, monstrous, impossible Fae. Some were winged, some horned, some hooved. I even noticed a tail slinking out from under a cloak and wrapped around the staff its owner held. They were dressed in clothing like I'd never seen – not even on Scouvrel or the Fae who came to claim Hulanna.

The woman nearest me gasped as I emerged from the stone ring – but I was just as shocked as she was. Her yellow dress had panels in the skirt that held actual caged birds in a variety of colors from flaming red to the richest of peacock blue. The woman beside her – a dark beauty with gleaming polished ram's horns, wore a slinky dress of black living vines. They shifted and moved as I watched, changing shape and by turns covering or revealing her skin as they chose.

A male Fae snickered, holding up a fluted glass filled with a silver substance like molten metal. He lifted it in hands lined with dark brown thorns and drank, leaving a silver smear across his lips but his lizard-eyes never left mine.

All watched me with beautiful, greedy visages, like the old gods of the forest come to roost. This was a party of some sort, though they had frozen at my appearance, laughter cut off midtrill. Dancing mid-stride. Drinking mid-sip.

They froze as if I had brought winter with me and ensorcelled them all.

It was only then that I realized I still had my blindfold off.

I started to pull it up but Scouvrel stopped me with a word. "Don't."

"Wha –"

"A bargain is a bargain, Hunter," Scouvrel said in a choked voice. "Let the unicorn free."

I swallowed, nervous with all eyes on me, as if their sudden freeze had frozen me, too. I couldn't tear my eyes from them.

I fumbled for the latch as the Fae around me parted.

Behind them, a cliff rose up with something like a waterfall made of smoke tumbling down its face. Smoke rippled white and murky spilling like translucent milk from ledge to ledge in a seductively smooth way. It spread an enchantment over me like I'd never felt before so that I wanted nothing more than to sit down and watch the smoke spill from pool to pool.

At the bottom of the smokefall, smoke rippled and billowed out forming the shapes of horses charging, and great ships on the waves, dragons leaping, castles on fire, magnificent heroes and terrible villains battling with sweeping sword strokes and flinging fireballs. One Legendary scene melted into the next and the next as the smoke rippled through the party, hugging the ground as it sloped down to where we were, and rippling between the legs and up the skirts of the gathered Fae.

And on the top of that hill standing in front of the smokefall, revealed as the crowd parted, and more beautiful than I remembered – more beautiful than I thought possible – was my twin sister.

On one side of her, against a gnarled tree wreathed in smoke, hung Olen's father, nailed to the tree with bronze spikes through his shoulders. His mandolin lay crumpled at his feet and his eyes were glazed over, head bowed down in great pain.

I gasped, my gaze sweeping to my sister and the angelic smile on her face and then to her other side where another twisted tree glowed in the smoke. Spiked to that tree in the same way Chanter had been, was my father. His eyes were fiery with defiance, but his own head hung down as if he could no longer lift it and he did not speak, though he must have seen me.

Horror filled me, leaving a sour taste in my mouth and making my limbs tremble like rustling leaves.

"Alastra," my sister said, her smile as innocent as a child's. "One came through the portal, now another one may leave. But which one? Hmmm? Which one? The one in my hand?"

She spread her hands so that they lay on the heads of Olen's father and mine and around me, I heard Fae laughter at the great joke, the great cruelty of taunting them with freedom.

But surely, this couldn't be Hulanna. Not my twin sister with the dreamy eyes and the sweet smiles. Not my friend. She could be selfish and petty, I knew, but she could also be loyal and brave. This wasn't her. This wasn't who she was.

But with the taste of apple in my mouth, I said clearly, "I want you to free Father."

I was still holding the key in my hand. I shoved it in my pocket and as if that had changed something, her eyes turned feral and she laughed with her Fae friends.

"Done."

Olen's father vanished as I gasped, betrayal whipsawing through me.

"Well," she said with a wry twist to her mouth. "Someone's father."

"Please," Scouvrel whispered. "The bargain."

I needed to concentrate on Hulanna. I needed to find a way to free my father. What I didn't need was Scouvrel distracting me right now.

I opened the cage.

The unicorn leapt out, growing to full size again as it pawed the earth, stamping the crumpled crimson leaves underneath and snorting into the snow-flecked air, its breath pouring out like a smoke waterfall. Red blood flecked its sides from where Scouvrel had stabbed it over and over in his fight for dominance. Scouvrel glowered from the unicorn's back, needle in hand – as large as a rapier now. He was more beautiful than ever, a haunting darkness filled his eyes and his smoky wings swirled around him like pillars of hell.

And yet, my eyes were not on him in all his otherworldly glory. My eyes were on my father, on the barely contained fury in his eyes as he looked toward us. I had meant to free him. I had meant this sacrifice to be *for* something.

Carefully, I set down the cage and drew my bow from the quiver, stringing it in a smooth motion.

"Knave of Courts," my sister whispered, her eyes on Scouvrel and a deadly tone to her voice. From behind her, her green-eyed Faerie mate stepped out to join her side.

He smiled broadly. "Always you are welcome in the Court of Cups, Knave, but what is this game you have brought to us?

The unicorn settled and snorted as if it had suddenly lost all its vicious will and had become nothing more than Scouvrel's mount.

"A game all my own, Lord and Lady of Cups," he said with a laugh and lightning-fast his needle – now the size of a sword – jabbed out and flicked the cage from the ground in front of me. I gasped as he caught it, spinning through the air, pulled a hair from the unicorns head, wrapped it around the handle and looked at me with an expression of grim pity.

He surprised me with a sudden mischievous wink, as if the pity had only been in my imagination, and then – quicker than thought – everything changed. The world seemed to shift and then I was standing on a massive ball of cloth – stamped and trampled by muddy hooves and bloodied until it barely looked white.

And I looked out past iron bars as fat as my forearm at the world beyond which suddenly looked much larger.

I gasped again – like a fish trying to breathe in the air, my eyes just as wide, my heart hammering just as hard and de-spair creeping through me like the picture-smoke through the woods.

A bright green eye – huge as a barn door – looked through the cage at me, and Scouvrel's voice said, "I'd put the bow away. That arrow won't be of much use to you now. It's barely the size of a splinter."

"What game is this?" I asked, echoing the Prince beside my sister and Scouvrel laughed.

"I play my games for blood and bones, hearts and souls ... and sometimes kisses." His final wink left me more unsettled than anything else.

I was utterly at his mercy.

And I had not been very kind to him when he was at mine.

Fear, like nothing I'd ever felt before weakened my belly until I leaned to the edge of the cage and vomited.

Souvrel cursed and I realized my vomit had splashed down the side of his white unicorn's mane. But the Court of Cups only laughed as the unicorn reared again and Scouvrel called to my sister, "Find me if you can, Lady of Cups, and then we'll have a true game!"

The unicorn was leaping forward before his front feet hit the ground.

My gaze sought desperately for my father's, locked with his, and held our shared look of agonized despair as the unicorn sped away and eventually, he became too small to see at all.

My heart was like a bird fluttering in a snare. My breath fluttered, too. Barely there at all. I was going to faint if I didn't get myself under control.

"It was very convenient for me that you wanted to come to the Faewald, Little Hunter," Scouvrel said as I clung to the bars, watching my very best efforts crumble like the cheese to which Scouvrel had compared the world. "If you have any more bright ideas like that, be sure to share them. I'm always up for a game."

"Truth or Lie?" I managed to gasp. "I won't leave this place alive."

"Truth," he said, and he almost sounded sorry about it as he rode through the velvet darkness on the back of a bleeding unicorn.

"Truth or Lie," he asked, his voice sounding pained. "You'll kill me if you can."

"Truth," I agreed. And I felt my fear begin to lick away as fury took its place, fuelling me, giving me the strength to stay focused.

I was going to make Scouvrel pay for this.

And then then I was going to hunt down Hulanna and free my father.

That was all I'd wanted when I came here – but suddenly it wasn't enough. Not even close. Because when I was done with them, I was going to end every one of these other Fae and every one of their Faerie tales. I wasn't going to leave this place until no human ever heard the name "Fae" again or knew what it meant. Until this whole species was no more than a silly tale told by grandmothers to frighten spoiled children.

"Be careful, Little Hunter," Souvrel whispered. "You're beginning to look like a Faerie with that expression on your face."

READ MORE OF ALLIE Hunter's story in Fae Captive, Book Two of the Twisted Fae series.

Behind the Scenes:

USA Today bestselling author, Sarah K. L. Wilson loves spinning a yarn and if it paints a magical new world, twists something old into something reborn, or makes your heart pound with excitement ... all the better! Sarah hails from the rocky Canadian Shield in Northern Ontario – learning patience and tenacity from the long months of icy cold – where she lives with her husband and two small boys. You might find her building fires in her woodstove and wishing she had a dragon handy to light them for her

Sarah would like to thank **Harold Trammel** and **Eugenia Kollia** for their incredible work in beta reading and proofreading this book. Without their big hearts and passion for stories, this book would not be the same.

Sarah has the deepest regard for the talent of her phenomenal artist Luciano Fleitas who created the gorgeous cover art that accompanies this book. Without his work, it would be so much harder to show off this story the way it deserves!

Thanks also to the Noble Order of Female Fantasy Authors who keep me sane – sort of.

And for my beloved husband, Cale and sons Neville and Leif who are endlessly patient as I talk to them about bookish passions.

[www.sarahklwilson.com](https://www.sarahklwilson.com/bridge-of-legends)[1]

Follow Sarah to keep up with fun updates:

---

1. https://www.sarahklwilson.com/bridge-of-legends

[INSTAGRAM](2)
[FACEBOOK](3)
[AMAZON](4)
[NEWSLETTER](5)

---

2. https://www.instagram.com/sarahklwilson

3. http://www.facebook.com/sarahklwilson

4. https://www.amazon.com/-/e/B0064MSJRE

5. https://www.subscribepage.com/dragonschoolfansjoin2

www.ingramcontent.com/pod-product-compliance
Lightning Source LLC
Chambersburg PA
CBHW070608310726
48982CB00001B/18